Hidden Lies

This is a work of fiction. Similarities to real people, places, or events are entirely coincidental.

HIDDEN LIES

First edition: December 25, 2016

Copyright © 2016 Kristin Coley

Written by Kristin Coley

Proofread by Carolyn at Particular Proofreading (hollycat50@gmail.com)

For all of the fans who love Addie and Jake as much as I do.

Chapter One

"It's freezing!" I complained, stomping my feet to keep them from going numb.

"Oh, suck it up." Carly shook her head, as a scarf desperately attempted to hold back her unruly mass of hair. "We're going to meet this psychic, even if we have to stand here all day."

I groaned, already over the idea. Carly thought every psychic and medium who advertised in the yellow pages was a fraud, and it was our duty to expose them. Personally, I couldn't care less, but she thought it was a great project for our criminal justice class. I thought she was asking for trouble.

"I don't think standing in the cold outside their place of business, which clearly states they're closed, is the wisest use of our time." My hands were shoved into my pockets, but the cold wind seemed to cut through every layer I had on, and I couldn't stop shivering. "Why don't you just ask me when he's coming back?"

"Oh," she said, looking sheepish at my question. "When is the fake psychic coming back?" I rolled my eyes at her persistence, even as the knowledge he wouldn't be back until Saturday came over me.

"Saturday. Now, let's go before I'm frozen to the sidewalk." My fussing had her moving, for which I was grateful. I could be curled up with Jake, instead of standing in the freezing cold, trying to satisfy Carly's desire to reveal fraudulent psychics.

"Where are we going?" Carly bounced down the sidewalk, seemingly unaffected by the cold, as I trudged behind her, wishing she was bigger, so she could block the wind.

"Uh, come on, slowpoke." She grasped my arm, tugging me forward. "So ... what's next on the agenda?"

"I thought I'd stop by Jake's and see him." I sent her a sidelong glance to see how that went over. Her expression was crestfallen, but she cleared it almost immediately.

"Oh, okay, that's great." I knew it wasn't, and felt a prickle of guilt. Jake and I had started dating after I graduated high school. Well, actually right after I turned eighteen. We'd met in my senior year, when a local boy had been kidnapped. My ability had allowed me to know where the boy had been taken, and I'd wound up enlisting Jake's help to rescue him. The entire situation had become a doozy of a story, but suffice to say, because of our age difference and Jake's job, we'd had to wait until I was eighteen to 'officially' date. At the time, it hadn't had a huge effect on my friendship with Carly, because she'd been preparing to go to college out of state.

In fact, she'd spent our freshman year at Millsap, a private college in Mississippi, while I'd gone to a local state college. We'd kept in touch through text and the occasional weekend home, so spending the majority of my time with Jake hadn't been an issue. However, Carly had decided to transfer to my school for sophomore year. While I'd been excited about this, our dynamic had changed, a fact it'd taken us both some time to get used to.

Where I'd spent most of my weekends with Jake, Connor and Jules, now I also had to split my time with Carly. They all knew about my ability—the way I knew the answer to almost any question, even things I had no logical way of knowing. She even knew about my dreams, the ones that occasionally predicted the future. She referred to them as psychic visions. You'd think a shared secret like that would give us enough in common that we could all hang out together, but Carly inevitably wound up feeling like a fifth wheel. With Jules and Connor dating, plus me and Jake, it tended to leave Carly out, so I tried to spend time with just her.

Occasionally, we'd have a girls' night and include Jules, but it was awkward. Carly hadn't gotten to know them like I had, since she'd heard about all the crazy events of my senior year, after-the-fact.

Now, in the winter semester of our sophomore year, we'd found an uneasy balance. Carly tried to be supportive of my time with Jake, time that seemed to come less often with his increased caseload, while I tried to carve out specific time with Carly between studying, classes, and Jake. It was slightly better, now that Carly and I shared a couple classes. We had an opportunity to hang out and discuss stuff between classes, instead of going in opposite directions.

The guilt was still there, though. I knew Carly was lonely. It was the main reason she'd come back home, and the fact I had a group of friends she wasn't a part of didn't help matters.

"Join us," I told her impulsively. I knew Jake wouldn't mind ... much. She gave me a disbelieving look, but I kept my smile fixed in place. She'd never become part of our group if we didn't include her.

"I'd rather not be the third or fifth wheel if Jules and Connor are there." Her expression was dejected, increasing my guilt exponentially.

"Really." My voice was more certain as I threw my arm around her shoulders. Carly was tiny, with her head barely reaching my shoulder, and I was only five foot four. "We'll make hot cocoa and play UNO." Those were two of Carly's favorite things, and to be honest, mine too. I adored Jake, but he was a terrible UNO player. I could tell by her expression she was caving, so I dangled the one thing I knew she couldn't resist in front of her. "Who knows? Danny might be there."

She shot me a hopeful look, her crush on Daniel Phillips well known to me. Daniel, or Danny, as I liked to call him, was the kidnapped boys' older brother. I'd never met him in the course of my investigation with Jake, because he'd been in protective custody then. But after everything went down, Jake had become friends with Danny.

Danny was a hard guy to pin down; dark and brooding, after everything he'd been through. The polar opposite of Carly, who had sunshine shooting out of her ass. Not that I would ever say that to Carly.

"Oh, well maybe we could play some UNO." Carly's hand went to her hair. "How's my hair look?" I bit back my laugh as I nodded, *seeing* her worry over the fact Danny could run screaming from her crazy hair.

"It looks good." And it did. Where it might have been viewed as a frizzy mess on anyone else, it suited Carly perfectly. She was as bubbly and big in personality as her hair was. However, her worry about it sending Danny running was valid, since the sight of her seemed to intimidate him. I winced at the thought. He'd had a difficult time after his brother, Samuel, had been kidnapped. There was a lot of guilt there, and while I hadn't known him previously, I imagined he'd always been somewhat reserved, much more so than Carly, which wasn't hard.

I drew out my phone to text Jake, letting him know I was coming over with Carly. A minute later, he replied with, "Cool. Everyone else is here." I groaned a little, catching Carly's attention, so I smiled reassuringly.

"Jake says great." I left out the part where everyone would be there, since that fact would have her backing out.

Something I didn't understand at all.

Carly was always the vivacious one, the one dragging me along to meet people, but when it came to Jake and the gang, she was the

8

opposite, more reserved than I'd ever seen her. I rubbed my eyes, uncertain how to make it all work.

We hopped into Carly's old Corolla to head over to Jake's. I was grateful she always seemed willing to drive me around. I'd purchased a car after high school, but my mom's car had been totaled a few weeks earlier, and she needed a car more than I did, so she was borrowing mine. I lived on campus, in the honors dorm, which was really nice, since they were like small apartments, and between Carly and Jake, I usually had a ride if I needed one.

It didn't take us long to get there, and as we chatted about one of our professors, Carly seemed to loosen up. My fingers were crossed that when Jake said everybody, he meant Danny too. I knew Danny occasionally felt the same as Carly when he was with us—a fifth wheel who didn't have a place in our group. With my ability, it was sometimes impossible not to have intimate insights into other people's minds, and often someone's mental response to a random question would surprise me.

We walked into the apartment, the door unlocked, since he was expecting us. I was immediately engulfed in a painful hug the second I stepped in.

"Mmph," I managed, hearing 'Addie' above my head somewhere. He finally released me, and I stumbled back.

"Connor." He ruffled my hair with a grin as I pursed my lips.

"Gonna get stuck that way." I glared at his sage advice, moving around him to be wrapped in another hug, this one causing me to smile. His strong arms cradled me, and his lips brushed against my icy cheek. I felt his lips curl into a smile as he asked, "Cold?"

"Not anymore." I snuggled deeper into Jake's embrace, happy to be with him. He obliged me by tightening his hold, rocking us gently. Reluctantly, I withdrew from his embrace, remembering

Carly. She was standing to the side, looking uncomfortable. I reached over and took her hand.

"You're gonna help me make the hot chocolate, right?" She flashed me a smile as Connor whooped behind us, "Hell, yeah. Hot chocolate is what I'm talking about."

"Can you make it without me?" she teased, well aware of my tendency to burn it when I attempted. I shrugged, unembarrassed by my lack of proficiency in the kitchen. I figured psychic abilities trumped cooking skills any day. Especially when your boyfriend happened to be a cop.

We headed into the kitchen, waving at Jules, who was curled up on the couch, as we passed by.

"Whoa."

"Oh, hi."

We came to a sudden halt, as we ran into Danny. He stood uncomfortably in the doorway of the kitchen, blocking our access. Carly was struck silent, twirling her hair on her finger. Danny looked everywhere but at her, or me for that matter. I finally broke the awkward silence asking, "How are you?"

He gave me a quick glance, a muttered, "Fine," his only response.

"Great." I dragged Carly around him, because she was apparently frozen in place at the sight of him. Don't get me wrong.... Danny was the epitome of tall, dark and dangerous, but Carly's reaction was borderline ridiculous. I was pretty sure I'd never been this stupid over Jake, and he was much better looking. Jake had these changeable hazel eyes and tousled caramel hair, whereas Danny was all dark angles. He kept his black hair buzzed short, and his brown eyes were so dark, they appeared black to me. He had a piercing stare, a perpetual frown, and I couldn't grasp

10

what Carly found so fascinating about him. They were polar opposites.

I put the pot on the stove, gathering the other supplies we needed, as Carly stood there in a daze. I shook my head at her reaction to him. She'd never exchanged more than a dozen words with him over the past few months, turning into this shy, reserved girl I didn't recognize when he was near. But as soon as he was gone ....

"Oh my God. Did you see him?" She peered at me with huge eyes. "He's so gorgeous. And soulful. Did you see his eyes? He's drowning in pain." It physically hurt me to stop myself from rolling my eyes at her. "I just ... he just ...." A deep sigh escaped her. "It's like there's this connection between us."

I bit my tongue hard to stop myself from saying, "Really? You've never actually had a conversation with him!"

She continued her gushing, thankfully taking over the hot chocolate making while she did. I hopped on a barstool, figuring I might as well be comfortable if I had to listen to her wax poetic about Danny. Honestly, he wasn't a bad guy ... anymore. He'd been on the wrong side of the law, when his brother was kidnapped, but he'd been trying to make it right. His decision to narc on his drug suppliers was what got his brother kidnapped. That decision had changed all of our lives, and Danny had been living under a dark cloud ever since. His darkness seemed to call to Carly, but it made me want to avoid him. His pain struck a little too close to home for me.

"Do you think he'll stay and play UNO?" Carly's question interrupted my musings, catching me off guard.

"I doubt it. He couldn't risk cracking a smile. His face might fall off." Her frown was ferocious as she waved a wooden spoon dripping with hot chocolate at me.

"That is so judgmental. You don't know what he's been through." My look had her backtracking. "Ok, maybe you do, but that still doesn't mean you can say things like that." She paused, and I could see she was really upset, making me feel about an inch tall. "I know you don't get it, and honestly I don't either. But there's something about him." I chewed on my lower lip, waiting on her to finish. "He needs people to care about him, and I understand that feeling," she finally said in a rush, turning back to the hot chocolate.

I slid off the barstool and gave her a one armed hug, laying my head on top of hers, because she was so short.

"You're the best kind of friend."

"Hey, is the hot ... oooohhhh, girls hugging …. Carry on." I shook my head, attempting to choke back my laugh, since it only encouraged the behavior.

"Connor …." My exasperation with him was clear, as he slung his arms around us.

"It's cool. I get it. Chicks are affectionate. No judging here. I mean, Jake is a lucky man."

"CONNOR!" Both of us shouted his name, and I elbowed him, perhaps a little harder than I intended, as I heard an, "Oompff."

"Are you wearing out our welcome?" Jules entered the kitchen, giving Connor a peck on the cheek at seeing his pout. "I thought I'd come help you bring everything out." She grabbed cups from the cabinet, as familiar with Jake's home as her own. "Is he being disgusting?" She shook her head in mock disappointment. "I can't take him anywhere. You'd think by now he'd be better."

"Oh, I see how this is going now. You're ganging up on me." Connor crossed his arms over his chest, pulling his shirt taut over his muscles. I reached over and pinched a nipple, causing him to yelp. He and Jake had taken to working out together. Danny too, if

I wasn't mistaken. Jake didn't feel the need to flaunt his gorgeous body, but Connor was a different story. He took every opportunity to flex those hard earned muscles, and I loved to give him hell about it.

Jules laughed, familiar with our antics. She insisted Connor was my brother from another mother, since I treated him exactly how she treated Jake.

"It's ready!" Carly gave the cocoa one last stir as she clicked the burner off.

"Don't forget the marshmallows!" Connor called, dodging the towel Jules threw at him as he left the kitchen.

"How do you deal with him?" Carly asked, surprising me. She shook her head. "He's so … loud." We all burst out laughing then. Loud was a good adjective to describe Connor. Happy was another. Connor was like having a puppy in the room. Irritating at times, but lovable. I considered him to be the male equivalent of Carly. At least, Carly when she wasn't around Connor and the gang. I ladled hot chocolate into the mugs Jules set in front of me.

"I'm not sure," she replied to Carly thoughtfully. "He's different from me, and it works. I'm happier when I'm around him. He's the sun to my moon."

I smiled at the imagery formed at her words. They really were night and day different. Connor was a quintessential surfer boy, who happened to be stuck in the bayous of south Louisiana. Blonde, blue-eyed and tanned. Jules, on the other hand, had skin paler than my own, with a cascade of dark hair framing light blue eyes. They were striking together … when they weren't arguing. I laughed to myself as I added marshmallows to the mugs. Jules was focused and intense, whereas Connor was laughing and laid back. It caused more than a few arguments at times, but they seemed to thrive on them.

"That's so sweet," Carly gushed, her thoughts obviously on another dark moody soul. I sighed, fiercely hoping something would come of Carly's crush. I didn't like to see her disappointed and Danny, well, Danny deserved some happiness.

"So …." Jules stared at me, considering, and I knew she was debating about asking me a question. I recognized the *look*. You know, the one where someone knows you'll know the answer to the question they want to ask, but isn't sure they want to know the answer, even though they wanted to ask it?

Yeah, it hurt my brain too sometimes.

Carly stilled next to me, her own intuition sparking.

I arched an eyebrow at Jules, waiting for her to continue. She bit her lip, suddenly indecisive, unusual for her.

"Where's the hot chocolate?" We heard bellowed from the next room, and the moment was lost.

I shook my head, laughing. "No wonder he got kicked out of his apartment for noise violations."

Jules laughed with me. "I think that was an excuse to move in with me."

"Not a bad deal."

We loaded everything onto a tray and headed into the living room. Connor was in the recliner and hauled Jules into his lap as she walked by. I set the tray on the table and curled up next to Jake with my mug, finally where I wanted to be. The only other place to sit was the loveseat, and I watched Carly perch on it next to Danny. Their discomfort was obvious, but I couldn't figure out if it was attraction causing it, or something else.

"Danny, whatcha think of the new job?" Jake wrapped his arm around me, his other hand cradling the mug of cocoa. I sipped the rich brew, inhaling the scent of chocolate as I did. From Jake's question, I already knew Danny liked this job better than the last one. He'd been bouncing between jobs, finding it difficult to keep a job, with his history. Most were dead-end, pickup work, and he wanted something more long-term. He thought this one had potential.

"Good. I like it. Has potential." His reply echoed my own thoughts, not unusual, since I already *knew* his answer. "Couldn't have gotten it without you. I really appreciate your helping me with the TWIC card."

"Hey, man, I'm just glad it's working out for you."

"The welding class I took in high school is coming in handy, that's for sure." His expression never changed, but I sensed the tension in his shoulders as he mentioned the past.

"What are you doing exactly? Working at the shipyard, fixing the ships?" I was a little puzzled by his job, and used the questions to distract him.

"Yeah," he said, glancing at me and then away. I thought that was the end of it, but he continued. "When I started, I was loading the ships, but they need a welder to fix cracks sometimes. I had a little experience and was in the right place at the right time. It looks like I'll have an opportunity to apprentice with a guy."

"Wow, that sounds dangerous," Carly chimed in next to him. He turned his head slightly toward her, but didn't look at her directly, nodding.

"Yeah, it can be. Gotta be careful." He was a man of few words that was for sure. Good thing Carly liked to talk.

"What do your parents think of you working on ships? I bet they're proud of you. Transporting cargo down the river is so important to the town's economy and the State's! Having the port right here provides jobs, and we need skilled workers to keep the ships moving. It sounds like it would be a good job, and not one just anyone could do." Carly's chatter kept her from noticing the

15

pained expression that crossed Danny's face when she mentioned his parents. I shot a look to Jake, and he gave a slight shake of his head. I knew he'd been trying to get Danny to go see his parents, but he kept refusing. His guilt over Samuel wouldn't allow him to contact them. We all knew it was foolish. His parents were desperate to see him and asked Jake for information about him regularly.

"Did you hear about the missing girl?" Jules' question was abrupt, stopping Carly's babbling and catching all of our attention. A girl had gone missing from the campus earlier in the week, but beyond that basic information, her question left an eerie blank in my mind. Jake's arm tightened around me as Connor answered her.

"Yeah, we were supposed to be assigned the case, but the new captain decided to give it to O'Reilly and Nash instead."

His disgruntled expression made it clear what he thought of this, and it didn't escape me he referred to the captain as 'new'. It'd been over a year since their captain was replaced, but they still both referred to him as 'new'.

"He's got his reasons."

Jake attempted to pacify Con, but I knew he wasn't happy about it either. With my ability to know the answers to questions, I'd helped them work cases often over the last year. It made their track record for closing cases stellar, and their conviction rate was one of the best in the State, because they had airtight cases. Jake's desire to help had him digging through old missing person cases, and together, we'd brought closure to a lot of families. You'd think with their dedication they'd be the captain's favorites, but that wasn't the case.

"Yeah, he thinks we're narcs." My eyes met Jules's at Connor's words. We both knew where his bitterness came from.

"Con …"

"What about the missing girl?" Danny's question was insistent, and I *knew* it stemmed from his brother's kidnapping. We shared that much. Missing people hit both of us hard.

"I don't know all the details, since it isn't our case, but it looks like a freshman went missing from the college. The parents are insisting its foul play, but there hasn't been any evidence of foul play. She could have just taken off." As difficult as it had been for me to believe, I knew what he said was true. We'd worked a couple missing people cases where they wanted to stay missing. They had their reasons, and for all we knew, so did this girl.

"But on the chance it was by force," Jake nudged me, drawing my attention. "I want you to keep an eye out and your Taser on you." His protectiveness could be overbearing at times, but I knew my getting shot last year was the catalyst for it. I shuddered. Getting shot once was enough for me. It had hurt like a son of a bitch.

"Was the girl kidnapped?" Danny's blunt question caused simultaneous, but completely separate reactions in me. One, I was suddenly aware he knew about my ability … how he knew was another question. Two, she had been kidnapped, and her terror was suffocating me.

Chapter Two

My eyes rolled up in my head, as the sensation of a gag in my mouth made me want to gasp for air, but it was the absolute terror which paralyzed my lungs and made breathing impossible.

"Addie," his voice sounded miles away, but the desperation in it tugged at me. "Answer me. Breathe shallow breaths. Remember when you got the wind knocked out of you? Tiny breaths, and it'll come back." His voice faded as tears pricked my eyes.

My eyes blinked back open slowly, Jake's face filling my field of vision. He looked scared, and it took a second for me to understand why. Then the memory of her terror rushed in, and I could feel the choking sensation attempt to take over again. This time, I was prepared and pushed it back. It had less power now, because it was a memory. I struggled to sit up, finding myself lying on the couch. Jake helped me, sliding behind me, so I reclined against his chest. He wrapped his arms around me tightly, understanding instinctively that I needed the reassurance of his presence. Connor was kneeling on the other side of the couch, his arms draped over the back as he observed me anxiously. His hands twitched, wanting to touch me, but unsure. I clutched the hand closest to me and squeezed.

"I'm okay," I murmured, even though we all knew it wasn't okay. I'd never had a reaction that strong. I wasn't entirely sure, but thought I must have passed out from hyperventilating. Her fear had overwhelmed me, short-circuiting my own body's basic functions.

"I'm so sorry. I had no idea. I suspected you had some ability, but I didn't know it would cause this," a male voice said beside me, and I was startled to see it was Danny kneeling next to me, his face full of more emotion than I'd ever seen on him. Jake snarled behind me, and I knew he blamed Danny for what happened.

I managed a weak chuckle, "No one could have predicted this." Jake's tension radiated through me. "Jake, relax. I'm okay. Really. It's not his fault. It's no one's fault. We couldn't know how his question would affect me."

"But we do know. We would have been more careful," he argued, obviously not ready to let it go.

"But he didn't know, and this is the least of our problems." I could feel him about to interrupt me and cut him off. "That girl was taken, and she's in danger."

Jake and Connor exchanged glances over my shoulder as Carly leaned over Danny's shoulder and said, "Welcome to the weirdness."

My faint smile was more real this time at witnessing Carly be Carly. Jules sat down on the end of the couch facing me.

"How bad?" Her question was meant to ask how I felt, but held an underlining question I was pretty sure she didn't intend.

A vortex opened inside my mind, a black gaping maw waiting to devour us all. The dark was so complete, it was dizzying. Once the sensation passed, my reply was shaky.

"Bad."

They were all staring at me now, and I could feel a light sheen of sweat on my face. It almost felt like motion sickness had overtaken me, but I was still sitting on the couch. I'd been through some ugly stuff when Danny's brother had been kidnapped, but nothing compared to the darkness I'd just experienced. I didn't know what it meant. A thought slithered in before I could stop it … *was that what death felt like?*

I forced the thought away, concentrating instead on what we could do now.

"Ask me some questions. Maybe we can figure out where this girl is." My voice trembled slightly, a weakness Jake perceived instantly.

"No."

The one word was dangerously calm, a warning as well as a command. It brooked no argument, and none was given. A squeeze of my hand startled me, and I glanced at Connor. His smile was sympathetic, but determined.

"He's right, psychic girl. You're not looking so hot. Let me go and see what I can dig up on this case the old-fashioned way, okay?" I wanted to protest; tell them I was fine, and we needed to do this, but I couldn't. The terror from the last few minutes had shaken me, making me reluctant to do anything that would bring it back. He saw the answer on my face and nodded. He was keeping his face intentionally blank, but I saw the quick flicker of his eyes toward Jake. He was worried. They all were, and I knew they should be, but not over me. I hadn't been able to articulate it, but something horrible was coming. Of that I had no doubt.

"Guess that's our cue." Carly squeezed Danny's shoulder, prodding him to get up. His expression was pained, and I knew he blamed himself. I tried to give him a smile, but it didn't seem to help, because he looked more upset. Carly kissed my forehead. "I'd offer to drive you home, but I think you should stay here."

There was a rumble of agreement from behind me at her words. Jake's arms formed a protective wall around me, and I had no desire to leave their safety at the moment.

"Daniel." The softly spoken word froze everyone in place. Jake was a mild-mannered guy, but he tended to be overprotective when it came to me. I hugged the arm he had wrapped around me, hoping he didn't say anything that would damage his friendship with Danny. I might not always understand the connection they had, but I respected them both and it wasn't Danny's fault.

Danny paused, resolve written all over his face. He would accept whatever Jake said, because he thought he deserved it. Connor clapped a hand on Jake's shoulder, warning him or backing him up, I wasn't sure.

"We're good." Jake held out his free hand to Danny, and he clasped it in some weird bro handshake I didn't understand. "If everyone can make it back here tomorrow, we'll go over what we learn. See if we can figure this out." He regarded Danny. "Explain."

Danny nodded slowly, understanding he was being invited in completely, if he wanted it.

"You want the cliff notes version before then?" Carly looped her arm through his, and he peered down at it in shock. She ignored his look and tugged on his arm. "Come on. You can tell me about welding, and I'll tell you about Addie."

Within seconds, everyone was gone, and I was alone with Jake on the couch. He sighed deeply and leaned back, pulling me with him. We laid there, his even breaths matching mine, my body cradled within his larger frame. I tucked my feet in, wanting every part of me surrounded by him. Slowly, I felt calm returning to me. The horror was still there, but manageable now.

"She's terrified and it overwhelmed me." The words came now, where they wouldn't earlier. Jake twitched and his hand came up the stroke my arm. "At least I hope she's terrified." I didn't say my other thought, that I hoped she wasn't dead, and I was feeling what she'd felt. Jake seemed to understand, humming gently. "But that wasn't the worst."

He shifted me around, turning me as if I weighed nothing and forcing me to meet his eyes. "What do you mean? There was more?"

"Jules." Her name escaped me, and horror crossed Jake's face. It took me a second, and then I understood. "No, no." I shook my head, reaching up to touch his face. The rasp from his stubble brushed my palm as I cradled his jaw. "It's what she asked me. Nothing will happen to her." Even as I said the words, though, I wondered. She'd been the one to ask me. Did that mean she would be affected? Or was it only the question that had triggered the void? Jake could see the turmoil on my face, and my name was a groan coming from his lips.

"Addie."

"I don't think it's her. I don't know what it is honestly." The very depth of the unknown frightened me, and I squirmed closer to him, burying my face in the curve of his neck. He tightened his arms around me, pulling me closer.

"Can you explain what it is you know? Saw? I'm in the dark here, babe." His choice of words sent a shudder through me, and he felt it. "What is it? Please." His words were tight with worry, and I shoved back the cloying fear, angry at my own weakness.

"She asked 'how bad' and her question … it opened a door in my head. But there was nothing there." I faced him, unable to blink, even as my eyes burned. "It was a void, a blackness without end. The sheer absence of anything made me sick." My head shook as I opened my mouth, trying to get the words out. "I don't know what it means. Death?"

A fierce resolve came over his face.

"No." His eyes burned with determination. "Not death. There is absolutely nothing we can't beat together. Do you understand?" I nodded, needing his conviction. "We've faced death and bad visions. This is no different." It was different. It felt different, but I wouldn't say it. We would need everything we had to face whatever was coming. I didn't tell him the door was still in my mind. It was as if Jules' question had made me aware of it. I'd managed to shut it, but that didn't mean it had gone away.

Later, I woke to the sound of Jake murmuring into the phone. I was on the couch, wrapped in a blanket. I must have fallen asleep in Jake's arms at some point, but he wasn't with me now, and looking around, I saw him pacing in front of the window. His voice was low, an attempt not to wake me, I was sure. He shoved a hand through his hair, the movement a familiar one to me, as he did it when he was frustrated with a case.

"There has to be more." I caught the words, even as he tried to keep his voice down. "We'll go back over the scene. We know there was foul play now. We'll search her dorm room, car, everything." He listened for a second before exploding. "I KNOW IT ISN'T OUR CASE!" He glanced over at me, and I held still, listening as he lowered his voice again.

"This is bigger, Con. She saw something that scared her. Scared ADDIE. That doesn't happen. Something about this case." He paused, collecting himself. "I'll talk to the new captain. See if I can get the case transferred. Pull strings or something. Don't you play poker with Nash? Maybe they'll voluntarily hand it off to us." He listened, and I heard the gratitude in his voice when he said, "Thanks, man. You don't know what it means to me. Yeah, I'll talk to you tomorrow."

He ended the call, and I sat up. A flash of white revealed his smile in the semi-darkness.

"Did you hear everything?" His question was gently teasing, and I smiled back, the knowledge of what I hadn't heard forming in my mind at his question.

"They don't have anything, do they?" He heard my disappointment.

"They didn't know she wasn't missing voluntarily," he replied, sitting across from me and enfolding my hands in his. "It's a difficult line. You know that. There were no obvious signs she'd been taken against her will."

"But she *was*." I looked away from him, frustrated, but not with him. He hadn't said anything we didn't already know. It was one of the worst parts of a missing person case. Sometimes, you didn't know why they disappeared and adults were the worst. Resources were rarely allocated to look for them, because people went missing all the time, and there were more important cases. People like Deidre easily slipped through the cracks.

"Deidre. That's her name."

"Yeah, Deidre Martin. Nineteen. Brunette, five foot seven, roughly a hundred and sixty pounds. Last seen Tuesday night around five, heading to the library. That's all we know at the moment."

"She's my age." Jake dragged me toward him, brushing a rough kiss against my forehead.

"Yeah, I know."

It wasn't difficult to sense his worry. The idea of girls being kidnapped from my campus wasn't comforting. I thought about bubbly Carly and felt sick. What if it was her?

"We know she was taken. We can go back, start over, and find what was missed. Some evidence exists." I wasn't sure if Jake's words were meant to reassure me or himself, but they did remind me.

"Fish." I felt his gaze on me, so I peeked up at him. "I smelled fish, like fishy fish." He was staring at me, uncomprehending. "She smelled fish; fishy water maybe? I didn't realize it at first, the terror was so strong, but there was a distinctly fishy smell."

"Maybe where she was taken. A fishing camp, somewhere in the bayou—"

"Pretty much anywhere in south Louisiana?"

"It's more than we had," he reminded me. "Everything counts now. Every scrap of knowledge we can find. We'll find her."

"Alive?" I swallowed hard, unable to shake the fear we were already too late.

"Alive." He was confident, and his confidence boosted my own.

"What time is it?"

"Nine," he answered, glancing down at his watch. It was the one I'd given him for his birthday. It was a basic leather watch, inexpensive, but he wore it every day. "Do you want me to drive you home? Or stay here tonight?"

I leaned against him, "Stay." I felt the rise and fall of his chest as he exhaled, tightening his arm around me again.

"Good. I'm not ready to let you go."

Chapter Three

The weight of his arm almost knocked me down and it caused me to stumble. The arm tightened, keeping me upright as I tugged earbuds out of my ears.

I gave him a questioning look, wondering what he was doing on campus.

"There's a kidnapper on the loose. We don't know what his motives are. I'm on bodyguard duty." Connor flashed me a wide grin as he gave me a little shake.

"Fantastic," I muttered, not trying to hide my sigh.

"Oh, come on. We haven't had any time together."

"And whose fault is that? You keep your tongue stuck down Jules' throat. I don't see either of you!" I pinched his stomach, or attempted to, but there wasn't much to pinch. A cold wind had me tucking myself against him. If nothing else, he was a good wind block.

"Uh huh, like you don't do the same with Jake. Or you're hanging out with Carly." I didn't miss the hint of jealousy I heard when he said Carly's name. "When's your next class?"

"Two," I replied, already figuring I'd have to adjust my plan to study during my four-hour break between classes. I gazed longingly toward the library, the *warm* library. It didn't stay cold very long in Louisiana, but when it was, it was a bitter, icy cold that cut through any layer of clothing. I didn't relish the idea of staying out in it any longer than necessary.

"Excellent. We have time then." He whistled, tucking me in closer to him as he steered me toward the parking lot. *At least the car would be warm*, I thought to myself, not even bothering to ask what we were doing. Knowing Connor, it could be anything. Out of everyone who knew about my ability, he'd given me the hardest time about believing it, but he also happened to be the one who saw the most possibility in it. Granted, they weren't always the most ethical possibilities.

He cranked the heat as soon as we got in the car, seeing me shiver.

"Jules talk to you?" he asked me abruptly as we sat in the idling car.

"Whoa," I replied, giving him a wide-eyed stare. She hadn't talked to me, not about what he was asking me about. I blinked at him, uncertain of what I thought about this new development. "Not about that." A thought occurred to me as I remembered Jules unusual hesitation the previous night. "Maybe she intended to last night, but ... have you talked about this?" My finger wiggled around in a circle at him, and he shrugged.

"Something about it might have slipped out."

"Slipped out?" My disbelief was appropriate, considering the subject matter.

"Mentioned? In passing, but it felt right."

I blinked at him, "Does Jake—" He interrupted me before I could complete the thought.

"NO!" He relaxed a bit, giving me an apologetic look. "I didn't mean to shout, but I've barely wrapped my head around it. I mean, is it the right time? Am I jumping the gun here? Should we wait? Is she on the same page as me? I think she is, but this is big."

"Hold up." I pressed my fingers to my forehead. "Head rush."

"Ooh, sorry. I didn't mean to ask so many questions."

"It's alright, but have you *talked* to Jules? I mean that's kinda key when talking about marriage."

"It was one of those offhand comments you make. Ya' know?" I didn't know, since the word marriage rarely crossed my mind, let alone my lips. He caught my look and frowned, "Okay so maybe you don't, but it'll happen eventually. And I don't envy Jake with that proposal."

I glared at him.

"We're not talking about me and Jake. We're talking about you and Jules and MARRIAGE. This is a big deal."

"I KNOW."

We stared at each other in silence for a few minutes.

"I need a drink," I finally muttered, my head starting to hurt from all the questions he'd asked and the implications I could see.

"Alright." He put the car in gear and eased out of the lot.

A few minutes later, he turned into a gas station. I headed straight over to the fountain drinks and poured myself thirty-two ounces of Diet Coke. I sipped on it as I met Con in line.

"Which ones?" I glanced over at the lottery case behind the checkout lane. We'd perfected our shorthand over the months, after he'd finally persuaded me to start buying lottery tickets with him. I couldn't predict lottery numbers, no matter how often he asked me what the winning numbers were, but scratch offs were another matter altogether.

"Bayou Bucks. Four of them," I answered, sipping on my drink, even as he choked.

"Four! Those are ten bucks apiece. Do I look like I'm made of money? I earn a cop's salary," he grouched at me, pulling out his wallet to see if he had the cash.

"Go big or go home," I told him with a smirk, knowing the ticket was worth it. "You're getting my drink too."

"Yeah, yeah."

We made it to the front of the line, and Connor asked for four of the Bayou Bucks scratch offs, paying for my drink and a bag of peanut M&M's, while he was at it.

Once we got to the car, he handed me the scratch offs. It was a game we played. I told him which ones to buy. He bought them, but refused to scratch them. He always gave them to me to scratch, still under some impression I was a lucky charm and not just psychic. I scratched them methodically, making sure I got the entire box before handing the ticket to him. I saved the best for last, enjoying watching him wait.

I laughed as he figured out how much he'd won.

"Hell yeah!" He seized me in an exuberant hug, giving me a smacking kiss on the head. "I can buy a ring with that kind of money."

His words brought us right back to why we'd stopped there in the first place. I sighed and he frowned at me, his face sad.

"Don't give me the puppy dog eyes!" I waved my hands at him, closing my own eyes against his look.

"You sighed! That's not a good sign. I don't want to know Jules doesn't feel the same way. It causes the puppy dog face."

I started laughing at his words and then punched him on the arm. "Just because I sigh, it doesn't mean it's bad. It only means I took a deep breath. And maybe I'm sad, but not for you. For me."

He appeared confused at first, then his face cleared, and he gave me a knowing look. "Because you want it to be you and Jake?"

I groaned, laughing at his assumption. "No, because it means things will change. If you and Jules get married."

"If?" He was panicked at my use of the word if.

"You do have to ask her first. So yes, if."

"So I'm gonna ask her?"

"I don't know, are you?" I laughed, already knowing the answer, but giving him a hard time.

"You're a cruel woman," he said, giving me a mock frown.

"Don't I know it. And I'd wait till spring." He gave me a quick glance out of the corner of his eye, one side of his mouth raising up in a smile.

"Spring?"

"To ask her. A spring proposal and a summer wedding sounds right."

"This summer?" He blanched, and I collapsed into giggles at his expression.

"No, but for a man so ready to get married, you look a little scared."

"That's kinda sudden." He rubbed his chest, anxiety written across his face.

"Next summer," I reassured him. "It takes time to plan a wedding." He gazed at me, unsure, and I gave him a confident smile. He nodded, looking relieved, as he drove back to the school.

I convinced him that I really did need to study, but he refused to leave me alone at the library, insisting on sitting with me, even as I expressed doubt that I would be kidnapped in broad daylight from the *library*.

"You don't know. This person could be some type of weird sicko that gets off on girls reading books and shit."

"You have such a way with words. Why does Jules put up with you again?"

"Cause I'm a stud in the bedroom." His expression was dead serious, leading me to believe he wasn't joking. Knowing Connor, he probably wasn't.

"TMI."

"You asked." He smirked at me, and I laughed, until he said, "I could always ask you what Jules thinks of me in the bedroom. Remember that."

"Ugh, no!" I held my hands up in an attempt to ward the very thought away. He laughed at me, catching the attention of several girls studying a few tables over. I noticed none of them were irritated by his loudness, but instead had decided to check him out.

Not so subtly either. I glared over at them, and most turned back to their books. Connor caught me glaring and smiled, flexing his bicep.

"Don't like it when other girls appreciate my hard work?"

I switched my glare to him saying tartly, "I'm doing my best friend duty. Jules would have gone over there and told them something."

He gave me a sheepish look as he nodded. We'd both seen a jealous Jules in action, and it was something neither of us wanted to remember.

"You know we don't even know why Deidre was kidnapped. It could have been opportunistic." I was interrupted by Connor saying, "Look at you using big words." I rolled my eyes at him and continued.

"She could have had a stalker. We don't know. So you following me around is a little premature, at least until we have all the facts. You're not just following me around because Jake is worried about me and my reaction yesterday?" I was suspicious, because this felt a lot like protective custody, something I was very familiar with. I'd experienced it before with Jake and had no desire to repeat it. I always carried my Taser and actually had a concealed carry permit. Jules and I practiced at the shooting range regularly. We also took turns sparring with Jake and Connor, to keep our defensive training current. I made it a point to be able to take care of myself. I had no desire to ever feel the same helplessness I'd felt when I thought I'd lose Jake.

"You know he worries." Connor glanced up at me through his eyelashes, his expression commiserating, but resolute. I knew he'd probably heard it from both sides. Jules could be as ridiculously overprotective as her brother when it came to me.

"I do know! I worry about him every single day on the job." My attempt to whisper obviously didn't work when a guy at the next table shushed me. Connor turned to glare at the guy, and he decided to study elsewhere. Normally, that would make me laugh, but right now, I was aggravated at being seen as the weak one. Again.

"Yes, and it's unnecessary. You know I've got his back."

"I worry about you too!"

"Really?" I could *feel* his surprise at finding out I did actually worry about him and a certain warmth at the knowledge. I shook my head at him. "Of course I love you. You're the brother I never had. I worry about you as much as I do Jake. Your job is dangerous." I held his gaze, wanting the truth about his bodyguard duties. "Admit it. This is more about my fainting yesterday and the fact Jake thinks this is a repeat of freshman year."

He winced, giving me all the answer I needed. I sat back with a deep sigh, glaring at nothing in particular, as I recalled those first few weeks on campus.

I'd decided to live on campus in the dorms, even though I only lived a few miles from the school. I'd wanted the whole experience of college life. Jake had told me about his college years; with a few edits I was sure, because Connor's version didn't quite match Jake's. I was excited about the idea of living with a roommate, even if it wasn't Carly, like we'd always planned. The only problem was; I hadn't really considered the logistics of living on campus.

The constant barrage of people in classes, the dorms, and at the union, wore me down almost instantly. Living on a campus was vastly different from just attending classes at one. Questions came at me continuously. Just eating in the cafeteria was torturous, and I couldn't even escape to my dorm room. My roommate would ask me questions, or chat on the phone, asking her friends questions.

At one point in the quad, I'd become surrounded by a group of people having an animated Q&A study session. Their back and forth questions had overwhelmed me and caused me to collapse in the middle of the quad. Jake had gone ballistic upon finding out. Granted, the students had called 911 when I collapsed, and Jake heard the call come in. I knew it had scared him ... it had scared me. The idea that I couldn't handle even being on a college campus ate at me. What if I couldn't handle the real world? I'd never learned to turn my ability off. I wasn't sure it was even possible.

I hadn't told anyone of my difficulties living on campus, not wanting to appear weak, but after my collapse, Jake and Jules went into overprotective mode. I basically had one of them with me at all times, with Connor rotating in on occasion. Truthfully, that didn't help matters either. Most people didn't realize how often they phrased something as a question ... and really, that was all it took.

Ask a question and I'd know the answer. It might not always make sense to me, but it was still there. Most of the time, I learned things I didn't want to, or need to know. One of the things I did learn was that questions had layers. You could be asking someone something on the surface, but quite often there was an underlying question you didn't ask.

Jake insisted I move out of the dorm, because living there wasn't helping my situation. I'd known he was right, but resisted being told what to do. I wanted to make it work, but ultimately, I learned I couldn't live with someone who didn't know about my ability. It wasn't like I could tell her to stop asking questions.

The situation had come to a head when Jake couldn't get a hold of me on the phone one afternoon. He'd found me sitting at my desk in the dorm room, completely out of it. My roommate had been chatting on the phone, while I attempted to study. Her incessant questions about her boyfriend had sent me into an almost catatonic state. Jake had led me out of the room, and not knowing what else to do he'd brought me to his place. I didn't remember any of it, and that had scared me enough to move back home. He'd said after a couple hours I'd come out of the daze I was in, seemingly no worse for wear. But the fact was, we were both frightened by what had happened.

I told my mom I was homesick, which was why I was moving back home. Jules bought me earbuds to wear while I was around people. They worked out great, since they blocked me from hearing any questions not directed to me. It didn't look odd for me to be listening to music when I was walking between classes or eating at the union. It gave me back a sense of normalcy. The only thing missing from my college experience was dorm life, but I was wary to attempt it again. After enrolling in honors English for the next semester, I found it qualified me to live in the honors dorm, which had private dorm rooms for students. No sharing with a roommate meant I might actually be able to do it.

Jake had been hesitant, worried about what might happen, and I admitted I was concerned too. However, I wasn't willing to let it stop me. We'd experimented with my ability on several occasions, Jake always stopped if he thought it was too much, but we'd learned ways for me to manage a sudden influx of questions. I had faith I could handle a private dorm room. I insisted, and they helped me move in over winter break. I'd been there ever since, and life had been good.

Until now.

"This is not the same," I growled, frustrated at being perceived as weak again.

"I know that. I was there when you passed out yesterday, and back when school started. Very different, but the fact remains, he's worried about you. Hell, so am I." I glanced at him in surprise. "Yes, I worry about you too. You didn't see yourself. I thought you were dying in front of me; from something I couldn't see, hear, touch, or smell. The fear on your face ..." He paused and leaned over the table toward me. "I don't want to ever see fear like that again. Especially not from something I can't fight." He slapped his hand against the table causing me to jump at the noise. "What if someone had asked a random question in class about the missing girl and that happened?" I knew he didn't mean to phrase it as a question, but he had and I *saw* what could happen. If I'd thought Jake's reaction had been extreme, it had nothing on what would happen if I'd heard that same question in a class. "You're not weak, Addie. Understand: we don't think of you as weak. Hell, you might be the strongest person I know. But that just means when I see you vulnerable, I'm even more protective. And Jake is the same way. You can't fault him for that."

I blinked, his words making me see things differently. I bit my lip, ashamed at my reaction over their protectiveness. It was hard for me to see it as anything but confining, when actually, it was nothing less than what I would do if the situation were reversed.

"You're right." He appeared shocked, and I smiled. "Bet you don't hear that often." He chuckled, and I shook my head. "But you are right. I have been looking at this wrong. I'm blessed to have friends like y'all. Thank you."

He reached over and chucked me under the chin. "Anytime you want to tell me I'm right, I'm more than happy to hear it." I laughed, and he continued, smiling because he got the reaction he wanted. "But there are things we can do. Such as figure out what happened to Deidre. Was her kidnapping intentional?"

"Yes."

"Are there plans to kidnap more girls?"

The blackness swirled around me with his words, cries echoing at me.

"Addie!" Hands grasped my shoulders, shaking me. I blinked back to awareness to see Connor looking at me with a frightened expression.

"I'd say yes." I managed to tell him as he let out a shaky sigh.

"I think we're done for now."

I nodded in agreement, sick from the blackness.

Chapter Four

Carly wiggled her fingers at Connor as he deposited me at the door to my next class.

"Hey, how are you?" she asked immediately, her concern obvious as we walked into class. She'd texted me early this morning to check on me, but we hadn't seen each other since last night

"I'm good," I reassured her, leaving out my earlier episode with Connor. I had a feeling he was on his way to tell Jake right now, and I'd hear all about it tonight. I was about to ask her how it went with Danny when she started gushing.

"So you're okay. Yay! Danny and I talked forever last night. Well, twenty minutes, but that's like forever with Danny." I nodded, knowing I wasn't getting a word in, until she stopped. "I kinda filled him in on what happened back when his brother got kidnapped. Well, he knew, but he didn't know. You know what I mean? He didn't know how your *special ability* came into play." Her voice lowered when she mentioned my *special ability*. I hid my smile as she continued. "Anyway, he was really upset about what happened when he asked you the question. He had no idea it could affect you like that. I told him none of us knew. That was a pretty severe reaction. But he did promise he was coming tonight, so I get to see him again," she grinned, her eyes sparkling as she finished with a sigh.

"I'm glad he's coming by. I was a little worried yesterday that he wouldn't be back." I felt relieved, glad the episode hadn't put a fracture in his friendship with Jake.

Class started then, so we focused on our notes. This was our criminal justice class, and we both enjoyed it. I had a feeling we would both find ourselves in the criminal justice field, but in different capacities. My strength lied in discovering the truth, but Carly had a real future in prosecution ahead of her.

We headed out after class ended, both of us done for the day and starving, only to run into the last person I expected to see.

"Danny!" Carly immediately smoothed her hair at the sight of him, and I glanced around, wondering where Jake was. I couldn't figure out why Danny would be here without Jake, unless …

"You came by to see Carly?" I questioned him tactlessly, not thinking it through. He looked uncomfortable at my question, shifting a quick glance to Carly.

"Um, no. You actually." Carly's face was crestfallen, and I could have kicked myself. My thoughtless question hadn't taken into account just how far Jake's guard duty would go. If I'd had any doubts about Connor telling Jake about the earlier episode, they were gone now. Danny was still wearing his work clothes and getting several sidelong glances—definite interest from the female population, but the guys' looks were a bit less friendly. Danny looked like trouble standing in front of us, with his t-shirt dirty and torn, heavy steel-toed boots, and ripped jeans. His perpetual scowl didn't improve matters. Carly caught onto the rude stares, and as a guy strutted forward causing Danny to frown heavily, she grasped his arm and reached up to kiss his cheek.

"Hey, sweetie, glad you made it." I wasn't sure who was more stunned at her actions … me, Danny, or Carly herself. "Come on, let's go."

We walked toward the parking lot, and I huddled into my heaviest jacket, noting that Danny wasn't wearing anything thicker than his t-shirt.

"Aren't you cold?" I asked between chattering teeth. The cold seemed to taunt me, the wind slicing through me.

He shook his head, and a second later said, "Not really." The words sounded painful to my ears. It was like he wasn't used to talking and didn't quite know how.

"Why did you come to see Addie?" Carly piped up, her arm still looped through Danny's. He didn't pull away from her, not seeming to mind her being so close.

"Are you my new guard dog?" I bit out, swiping hair from my face as the wind tugged it from my collar. He snuck a quick look at me, nodding, and gave a faint smile. The sight was so unexpected, I almost tripped and fell. He reached out and caught my elbow, saving me.

"Clumsy, aren't you?" I gave him a sharp look, but he wasn't looking at me anymore, and my eyes narrowed. I thought he might actually be attempting a joke. "I wanted to apologize again for last night. Your reaction to my question was unfortunate and unforeseen. I am sorry." I blinked at him in surprise, and even Carly gave him a wide-eyed look. Those were the most words I'd ever heard him utter in a row, and more articulate than I would have thought him capable of. Danny gave the impression of brute strength, not elegant apologies. Apparently, I needed to quit assuming shit.

"No harm, no foul," I muttered, distracted by this new side of him. Maybe Carly had been right after all.

"And yes, I've been enlisted to guard duty. Jake would have been here, but he was called into a meeting with the new captain." My laugh was taken by the wind, but he still heard it and shot me a puzzled look.

"Jake and Connor have you referring to him as the 'new' captain as well," I responded, my steps picking up speed as I spotted Carly's car in the parking lot. As we reached her beat up Corolla, Danny shifted awkwardly.

"Do you need a ride?" Carly looked hopeful, and I knew she wanted an opportunity to spend more time with him. He nodded, and I immediately slid into the backseat before he could. Carly threw me a grateful look, as he reluctantly took the passenger seat next to her.

"So what's with the guard duty?" Carly cranked the heat up, for which I was eternally grateful, as I rubbed my hands together trying to create friction and warmth. Danny glanced back at me to see if I was going to explain, but I shrugged. He had a surprisingly unexpected way with words, and I wanted to hear his version of events.

"We suspect the kidnapping wasn't random or a one-time incident. This means any co-ed could be in danger, and with Addie's reaction when questioned about the missing girl, it was determined she should have someone with her."

"Diplomatic," I complimented him, and he shot me a look.

"But it was one question. We don't know if that would happen again. I mean, I definitely get the danger, if someone is snatching girls off campus, but again, so far, it's just been the one girl, Deidre, right?"

I nodded, knowing she was correct. So far, only one girl had been kidnapped, but I knew from my earlier talk with Connor, there would be more. And I suspected there had already been some we didn't know about from the cries that had echoed through the darkness.

"It was more than one question." Danny was relaxed against the seat, surprising me with how comfortable he was being in a car with the two of us. "Addie had a strong reaction to a question she was asked earlier by Connor."

"What?" Carly gasped as she spun around in her seat to look at me. Thankfully, we hadn't left the parking space yet, so her

40

reaction didn't endanger us. "You didn't tell me you'd talked to Connor. Well, specifically that questions were answered," she corrected herself, having seen me with Connor when he dropped me at class. "That's why Connor was with you. I thought he was talking to you about Jules. Why didn't you tell me?"

Her question lambasted me with her hurt and a strong feeling of being left out, neither of which had been my intention. With her telling me about Danny, which I didn't want to mention in front of him, and then class, I just hadn't had a chance.

"I was going to, but didn't have a chance yet. I knew we'd all be talking about it tonight." My attempt to soothe her hurt feelings didn't seem to work, as she glanced at Danny putting the car in gear. I knew what her look meant. Danny had known something before she did. I'd been with her and not taken the time to tell her something she thought was important. I rested my head on the seat, already exhausted by the day, and the worst hadn't even begun.

The minute we stepped into his apartment, he swooped me into the bedroom. My attempt to explain the day's incident was cut off by his mouth meeting mine. His lips were firm against my own, his touch fiercely possessive, but not hard. Our lips broke apart and met again as he gently kissed my lower lip, soft kisses interspersed with harder, more demanding ones. His teeth tugged on my lower lip, and I parted my lips, my hands clinging to his shoulders as he hugged me to him. His tongue swept over mine and I leaned into him, demanding entry of my own. Our tongues dueled, until we drew back with a gasp, heavy breaths the only sound in the room. His soft lips swept along my cheek, his nose bumping my ear.

"I love you. Forgive me for the bodyguards." My laugh came out in a shudder. He knew me well, his kisses a drug that usually had me forgiving him anything.

"Do you really think it's necessary?" I asked, placing a kiss against the side of his neck and hearing his own breath stutter for a second.

"I'd wrap you in cotton and only allow you out with an armed guard," he growled, his big hands running along my sides. "But you won't let me."

"Neanderthal." He gave a low chuckle against my ear, the soft puff of his breath sending a shiver down my spine as it brushed against my sensitive neck. He felt it and nuzzled the curve of my neck.

"I can try." I pulled back from him at his words and saw the question in his eyes. My hands tugged his face to mine, kissing him with everything I had, answering his unasked question. He meant well, even if he did tend to come off as alpha male. It was a struggle we'd always have, because I craved independence, but at times like this, I appreciated his tendency to be overprotective. I still couldn't admit how frightening I found the blackness. There were answers in it, I knew that—but what cost would it take to get them?

I released him, but his lips held mine, refusing to part with my own. I pressed my hands against his rock hard abs, my fingers stoking the deep ridges. He groaned as he finally rocked back.

"We have to go back out there. I can already hear the comments Connor will make." My smile was slow and apparently very sexy, because Jake leaned forward, kissing me hard.

"If you don't stop looking at me like that, I'm gonna say fuck Connor and keep you in here with me," he growled, sending a pleasurable shudder through me. We hadn't made love the previous night, Jake concerned more about my well-being. I appreciated the concern, but now I wanted comfort of a different kind.

I was about to say *forget them all* when someone banged on the door.

"Study time is over. Nobody has biology this semester." Connor called through the door, and as my eyes met Jake's, we burst out laughing. Leave it to Connor.

He hadn't forgotten how Jake and I met, any more than we had. Having a cop undercover at your high school, and pretending to be his girlfriend, while helping him bust a drug ring, tended to leave an impression. Our 'pretending' had quickly found us developing real feelings, feelings we'd had to suppress for multiple reasons, not the least of which was that Jake had a girlfriend at the time, and I was a minor.

"Well, I do believe that's our cue." He opened the door for me, and as I stepped out, he tugged me back against him, placing a kiss against my cheek. He released me just as quickly, and we continued down the hall.

"Your clothes aren't even rumpled. You did better than that in high school," Connor joked as Jules mouthed, "Oh my God," and slapped his shoulder. Carly giggled, while Danny smirked.

"Well, glad the gang's all here," I muttered, feeling a flush work its way up my cheeks. I definitely had to remember to punch Connor extra hard for that in our next sparring match.

My glare told him to be ready, but he only winked at me, completely unconcerned. He rubbed his hands together before saying, "Are we ready for a Q&A?"

Everyone made it a point to avoid his look, no one wanting to make the first move.

"Come on. Jules?" He squinted at her, and she met his gaze apologetically, denial written across her face.

"I can't." She shook her head. "You looked so terrified. I don't want to ask the wrong question."

43

"No, man. I did ask the question and I'm regretting it." Danny held up his hands, palms out, as Connor turned his gaze to him.

Carly bit her lip, looking resolved. "I'll ask." She swallowed hard, her eyes pleading with me not to make her do it. I shook my head, a sigh escaping me.

"Guys, I know it was bad, and I'm sorry it was. Trust me, I'm sorry. I don't want to go through it again either. But there's a woman named Deidre who is living in terror, and we are her only hope. We know there will be others, and I don't want to be responsible for that. So strap on a pair, and start asking." My voice sounded much stronger than I felt, for which I was grateful. I hoped no one noticed the white knuckled grip I had on Jake's hand, a grip he took without complaint.

"Where is Deidre White?" Whoever asked was male, but beyond that, I couldn't identify him, as the question consumed me. Normally, I would see an address, or even a pull toward the person, but this was different. It was like I was where she was, but the dark enveloped me so completely, I couldn't tell the difference between up and down. Claustrophobia clawed at me. I pushed it away, trying to focus on anything else, something that would give me a clue to where she was. The fishy smell was stronger, and with it I noticed a gentle rocking motion.

A sharp shake brought me back, and I was looking at Jake. His expression was pained, and I knew he wanted to pull the plug on this experiment. I didn't know what my own expression was, but I had a feeling it was bad, based on everyone else's.

"She's on a boat. And it's dark. So dark, she can't see anything. Besides that, I don't know."

"You couldn't lead us to her?" Danny's question was legit, since that was how I'd found his brother. I'd led Jake to him in the middle of the woods, instinct guiding me.

I shook my head. "No, there's nothing pulling me toward her. Not like the others I've found."

Jake sighed, his gaze meeting mine. I shrugged, understanding his fear, but unwilling to back down. "Can you remember anything else? Did you hear anything? Feel anything?" He asked me questions, trying to get a better idea, and I loved him for it. He might not always like my choices, but he supported them.

"I didn't hear anything." I cocked my head thinking. Something niggled at me, and I tried to pinpoint it. I closed my eyes, trying to remember the moment. "It's warm." My eyes popped open, excited, as I remembered. "Wherever she is, it's warm."

"Okay, she's on a warm boat, in the dark." Connor was only clarifying what we'd determined, but it was so vague, I frowned. Jake caught it and shook his head at me. "Is it dark because it's nighttime, or because they're keeping her in the dark?"

"They're keeping her in the dark," I murmured, positive of this.

"Maybe we're going about this wrong," Jules interrupted, leaning forward. "Maybe we need to ask about the person that kidnapped Deidre."

Nods all around had Jules focusing back on me.

"Can you tell us the name of the person that kidnapped Deidre?"

"Paul … no wait, Tyler." Connor was scribbling as I spoke.

"Is that his first or last name?"

"First. He used Paul, but his name is Tyler."

"What does he look like?"

"Skinny."

Danny chuckled, and even Jake flashed a small smile. Connor piped in, "You got more than skinny?"

I frowned at them. "He's skinny. Like small. I don't think he could easily kidnap someone."

"Maybe they're drugging them." Carly was curling her hair around her finger, looking uncomfortable as she became the center of attention. "I mean, my momma taught me not to take drinks or candy from a stranger. Because, you know, drugs." Her shrug was matter-of-fact, but her theory made sense.

"The guy's got dark hair. I'm betting it's dyed, cause that black is so not natural. Dark eyes, kinda pasty."

"Why would she go off with him?" Jules asked absently.

"Because she thought he needed help. And she didn't feel threatened by him." The knowledge was there, a subtle certainty, which had no explanation.

"Were you able to take over the case?" I remembered Jake was working on having the case reassigned to himself, but from his closed expression, I was going to guess the answer was no.

"Nash was willing to hand it off, but the new captain didn't go for it." Connor's lips flattened in disgust as Jake stood.

"His words, and I quote, *'Why don't you let someone else have the glory for once?'* He paced, his jaw tight with anger. "What the hell does fucking glory mean anyway? We are trying to solve cases, bring kids home …" He waved his hands around, angrier about this than I'd ever seen him. "Not win a damn prize."

"Jake." Connor's quiet tone caught Jake's attention. It was almost as if they'd reversed roles. "We work around him. This doesn't stop us." Jake nodded, rubbing his hand across his face. He sat on the ottoman across from me, a contrite expression on his face as he peered at me. I gave him a twisted smile, and stroked his cheek.

"You have a right to be angry about this." I clasped one of his hands in both of mine, "But Connor's right, and please God, let me stop having to utter those words." I stared up at the ceiling as I said it and heard a few chuckles. "We'll figure it out without the case file."

"Well …" Connor had a Cheshire grin and threw me a wink. "To keep my streak going … we do actually have access to the case file." I raised a questioning eyebrow, and Jake scrutinized him. "Nash might have slipped it to me on the DL. I owe him a case of beer at our next poker night, but I figured it was worth it."

"DL?" I asked, puzzled.

"Down low," Carly replied, looking smug. When I glanced at her, she shrugged. "I keep up with the slang."

"Awesome. Good job, Connor." I praised him reluctantly, already knowing the reaction I would get.

"What was that? I didn't quite catch it. Could you say it louder?" He cupped a hand around his ear and I shook my head.

"GOOD JOB!" I screamed in his ear, causing him to jump and everyone else to laugh.

After our laughter died, Jake stared at me warily. He had a question, one he didn't want to ask me.

"What is it?" He gave me a tiny smile, knowing I wouldn't let him get away with not asking. He glanced up through his thick eyelashes, his head tilted. Even after a year together, he had the ability to make my heart race. I closed my eyes for a second, to control my desire to lean over and kiss him. One make-out session a night was plenty for our friends.

"Is Deidre dead?"

The answer filled my mind and my eyes flew open. My smile was answer enough for them, and I threw my arms around him. I hated that question, but it was a necessary one. It was a relief to know she was out there, fighting, and made me all the more determined to find her, before the answer changed.

47

A week of babysitters had me close to pulling my hair out. Normally, I didn't mind hanging out with my friends, but seeing one of them standing outside of every class had gotten old. Even when I met Carly, they came with us. It rotated between Jake, Connor, Jules, and Danny, and it didn't seem to matter what I said. They were determined.

"Do you really think this is necessary?" It was Friday afternoon, and my companion for the day was Jules. "Nothing has happened. We don't have any more info about the Tyler guy or Deidre. No one else has been taken."

"That doesn't mean you relax your guard." Jules bumped me, smiling. "I know it's annoying. But none of us are willing to see anything happen to you."

"But why do you think it'll happen to me? Every girl on campus is at risk." My protest was borderline whining, since this was an argument I'd made more than once. She shook her head, repeating their stance.

"Considering how you've reacted to our questions; we don't want to take any chances. Plus, there's safety in numbers, and we're taking the opportunity to observe. You want to have police on campus." I glanced at her out of the corner of my eye.

"I don't think plain clothes officers have the same effect."

I heard a distinct growl coming from her and side-stepped in time to miss her punch. I laughed, unable to help myself. She squinted her eyes, daring me to say anything else. I shook my head, pulling open the door to the union. We made a beeline to CC's Coffee stand and ordered hot chocolates.

"So ..." she drawled, and I peeked at her over my cup, inhaling the rich chocolate.

"Are we actually going to have the conversation this time?" She grimaced at me, tucking her legs under her in the chair.

"I'm guessing Connor's already talked to you."

My lips curled up at the memory. She huffed, "Of course he'd beat me. You know it's very difficult having a best friend who's also good friends with my boyfriend." She gave me an irritated look.

"Kinda like when your boyfriend's best friend dates one of your best friends who also happens to be the sister of said boyfriend?" I smirked, pleased with myself. She mock-frowned at my cleverness and then dived into what was bothering her.

"Is he going to ask me?"

"Do you want him to?"

"Yes. But are we ready? It seems sudden, but I've known him for years. Is it too soon? It's such a big step, but it feels right. What do you think? What did Connor say?"

I blinked at her sudden influx of questions. The normally self-assured Jules was a rambling mess in front of me. I sorted through her questions, narrowing in on the only important piece.

"You already know your answer. Does the rest of it really matter?" She sighed, her expression of uncertainty worrying me. "Do you want to marry him?"

"Absolutely." Her one-word reply was confident, and I relaxed back into the chair. "It's just—"

"Really annoying when you don't phrase it as a question." It was her turn to smirk, but after a second it went back to contemplating.

"What if we're rushing into this?" I could see she thought it was too soon and people would talk. She was the type of person to have a five *and* ten-year plan. Connor had shaken all of that up, though. He was a fly by the seat of his pants and hope everything

50

worked out guy. Considering how close we'd come to losing him last year, I could get behind his zest for living life.

"What are you rushing into?" I asked her practically. She gave me a puzzled look. I arched an eyebrow. "Right now, you're dating. I don't see a ring on your finger, or a pregnant belly. You're a couple that have been together and are talking about marriage. Something couples do, I hear." I reached over and laid my hand over hers. "You're talking. That's all. Don't make this bigger than it is and scare yourself. Take it one day at a time." Her eyes were doubtful, so I pushed on. "Does he make you happy?"

"Yes. And angry and crazy and strong." She chewed on her lip. "He shakes me up; reminds me there's more to life than work. He's an incredible kisser. He makes me laugh, even when I want to beat him over the head. I can't imagine spending my life with anyone else."

I sipped my chocolate, inwardly relieved by her words. I'd known they had a lifetime love, but even knowing doesn't mean someone will make the leap. Jules had made the leap.

"Just remember, I'm maid of honor." She gazed at me, startled, and broke into a huge grin.

"Double wedding?"

Her question swirled through my head. There wouldn't be a double wedding in our future, but the shimmer of a pearl white dress flashed through my mind, along with Jake smiling at me.

I shook my head, in an attempt to clear my thoughts. My future wasn't up for discussion at the moment. Jules pouted, thinking the shake of my head meant no double wedding, which it did. I had no desire to take any part of her special day away from her.

Carly flopped down into the chair next to me, her hair even more wild than usual. We both stared at her in surprise as she frowned broodingly. It was not a natural look on her, and I opened my mouth to ask what was wrong, but she spoke first.

"What are y'all talking about?"

"Weddings." The word tumbled from my lips, and I hastily corrected myself. Weddings was plural and that was not the case. "Wedding, I mean. Specifically, Jules' wedding." Jules gave me a curious look, obviously wondering what was going through my mind. I ignored it, having zero desire to explain the flash I'd seen.

"What's wrong?" I wasn't sure Carly would answer me, but I should have known better.

"Danny!" She sat up straighter in her chair. "Seriously, the guy is …." She waved her arms around, words escaping her. A solid first for Carly. Jules hid her smile behind her mug.

"What did he do?" I finally asked, when it seemed like she'd given up on trying to find words.

"Nothing. He's done nothing."

I made a humming sound. I really had no idea what to tell her. The only relationship I'd had was with Jake, and it had its own special circumstances. Trying to give Carly advice on Danny would be like the blind leading the sighted. I flicked a glance at Jules, hoping she had some insight. Her shrug quickly ended that thought.

Carly sat there fuming, and I knew we needed to do something. This behavior wasn't Carly. She was a quick to anger, quick to smile kind of girl. Brooding and angst wasn't really her MO.

"I think we are in need of a girls' night." I grasped onto Jules suggestion with all the fervor of a drowning person lunging for a life preserver.

"That's brilliant." My smile was huge as I glanced between the two of them, catching Jules uplifted eyebrows at my excitement and the cautious smile on Carly. I nodded. "Yep, that's what we'll do. No guys, just girls hanging out and having fun."

"We can watch chick flicks on Netflix all night."

"Eat ice cream out of the carton."

"Paint our nails."

"Talk about the guys."

"Yeah, and someone needs to explain the weddings thing." Carly perked up with each suggestion, landing on the last one with a pointed look at me.

We woke up the next morning painfully aware we'd gorged on junk food and romantic comedies all night.

"I'm gonna have to go for a run tonight," Jules groaned, sitting up on the couch she'd crashed on when our chocolate high rivaled an alcoholic one. I shuffled from my bedroom, yawning, and tugging on the shirt I'd worn to bed. It was Jake's, and I'd stolen it the first time I'd slept at his place, back before we were even a couple. They were my pajamas—his t-shirt and sleep pants—and way too big, but it didn't matter. They were comforting and my favorite thing to wear.

"Ha," I replied to Jules' comment. "Like you need to run." She was tall and skinny, one of those women that could eat anything and never gain an ounce. Completely unfair, since I did actually have to watch what I ate and exercise. Granted, I avoided exercise when at all possible. If it wasn't for Jake and his insistence on regular sparring matches, I might be able to avoid it altogether.

She shrugged and glanced down at Carly, who was still passed out on the floor where she'd curled up with a blanket.

"Is she dead?"

"Nah, just a deep sleeper." I headed into my microscopic kitchen to turn on a pot of coffee. There was no doubt we'd all need it after last night. We'd stayed up late talking about the guys in our lives or lack of guys in Carly's instance. She'd declared she was over Danny and his insistence on ignoring her.

"Why now? He's been ignoring you for months," I'd asked her the night before.

"Thanks," she huffed at me. "Yeah, but we talked. I mean, it wasn't much, but we had a vibe. He could have pursued it. I don't want to be the one chasing. You know that never works." I shrugged, having no idea if it worked or not. "If he'd give me something. A text, a smile, anything! But he just does nothing. I can't work with nothing."

"Why don't you just ask him?" I made the obvious suggestion, and Carly skewered me with a horrified glance.

"What if he says no?" she finally stammered.

"Then you know."

"But it would be awkward."

"Yeah. I imagine he thinks the same." I lifted an eyebrow as she opened her mouth, and then closed it again.

"You and your logic," she muttered, giving me a narrow look.

The coffee started, the smell invigorating me, even as I waited for it.

"I understand her feelings for Danny," Jules commented, sitting cross-legged on the little couch. I glanced over at her as she studied the back of Carly's head.

"You have a crush on him too? What, am I the only one that thinks he's kinda scary and moody?" I reached into the cabinet and got down the only two mugs I had. We'd have to share whenever Carly finally woke up.

"No." She squinted to see what I was doing. "Is that the mug I gave you?"

"Yep, I need more, if I'm going to have guests," I joked, pulling the carafe to pour our coffee.

"I can handle that." She took the mug from me. "And no, I don't have a crush on Danny. I get what you mean about scary. He definitely has a 'don't mess with me' vibe." She shuddered slightly as she sipped the coffee. "I always forget you like the chicory coffee."

"You want cream?" I offered, turning back to the kitchen. Chicory coffee was strong, if you weren't used to it.

"Nah. It'll put hair on my chest. Or wake me up. One of the two." Jules smiled faintly. "I get the uncertainty Carly feels about pursuing Danny. I felt the same way about Connor. We'd known each other for years, but he's my brother's best friend. Who knew what would happen if it didn't work out? Talk about awkward. The fear of messing everything up is real. And Carly ..." She waved an arm at her. "She feels out of place already. Can you imagine if it didn't work out with Danny? Two people that already feel like outcasts in our group and they break up. It'd be like everyone was taking sides, or they'd leave the group altogether."

"What a cheerful thought on a Saturday morning. Thanks, Jules." I plopped down on the other side of the couch. "But what if it works out? Carly is obsessively interested in him, and I think he returns her interest, but both of them are letting fear hold them back. And I get it. Going into that warehouse to save Jake and Connor wasn't as scary as the first time I told him I loved him. Putting your emotions out there is terrifying."

Jules made the sign of the cross when I mentioned the warehouse. She was Catholic to the core, and firmly believed our surviving was due to prayer. I couldn't say I disagreed. That day was etched in my memory as one of the stupidest plans I'd ever had, and I knew Jake would agree. We'd taken a huge risk, when we went into save them from the drug lord who'd planned to kill him.

"Agreed, but not everything works out like you and Jake, little Miss Optimistic," Jules grinned, removing any hint of sarcasm from her words.

"Yeah, sometimes it works out even better, the future Mrs. Connor Hayes." We giggled at the thought. Something about the idea of a wedding sent a thrill through any girl and made her imagine her own wedding. The idea floated in that one day Jules and I might actually be family. I shook my head at the thought that Connor might actually be my brother-in-law one day.

"Alright, I have to go. I'm supposed to meet Natalie for brunch." Natalie was their sister-in-law, John's wife. "She said John and Tyler are having a father and son day." I nodded, knowing they did that pretty often. "Natalie said she had something she wanted to tell me. Pretty sure she's going to say she's pregnant."

"Want to ask me?"

"No, I'll let her tell me, but I'm almost positive that's what's going on. John is terrible at keeping a secret, and he's acting exactly like he did when they were pregnant with Tyler."

"That'll be exciting," I said, smiling at the thought of another little Kincaid around. My brow furrowed, seeing Jules' frown. "Or not exciting?" She caught my look and attempted to smooth her frown.

"No, no. It's exciting." She stopped, and I leaned forward, wondering what the deal was. She took a deep breath and then burst out, "It's just hard!"

I blinked, not expecting that.

"What's hard?"

"Babies."

"I can't say I have a lot of experience with them, but won't they be taking care of the baby?"

"Yes, but I'll have to see the baby. And her pregnant belly."

"Generally, yes, you would. Is that a problem?" I was extremely confused now, and felt like I was walking through a field covered in land mines. Something was going on that I had no idea about.

"It's nothing." She gave me a forced smile, standing up abruptly and walking to the kitchen.

"Jules ..." She spun back around, after depositing her mug into the tiny sink.

"I'm going. I don't want to be late for the big announcement." She tugged at her wrinkled shirt and jeans. "I should probably stop by the apartment and change." She gave me a firm stare and pointed at me. "And you stay here. No going off without someone with you. Understand?"

Her sincerity blasted me, and I found myself nodding. It was difficult to ignore the directive when you could understand the reason why so completely. She was truly frightened of something happening to me when no one was around to help.

She must have read the honesty on my face, because she nodded too and headed for the door. The second the door clicked shut, Carly's head popped up.

"Okay, so the baby stuff was weird. What was up with that?" She was gazing at the door and didn't see me step back into the counter. It felt like I'd been punched in the gut. Understanding buzzed through me and I blinked back tears. If I'd ever needed it, here was proof that it didn't matter how well you knew a person, you still didn't know everything, even if you had special gifts.

"I don't know," I managed to say. "I'm going to go and change. Coffee is in the pot."

I dragged clothes on in a daze, my new knowledge making me emotional. I wondered if Jake knew, but also knew I wouldn't ask him. Knowing something so intimate about a person, knowledge they hadn't shared with you, was a curse of my ability. It could give me an unfair advantage, or just make someone uncomfortable. Jules had dodged my question intentionally, and I respected her choice. She had the right to tell me when she was ready, if that ever happened. Her nerves about marriage made more sense though. I couldn't help wondering if Connor knew. I didn't think it would make any difference to him, but it was something he should know first.

I sat down on the edge of the bed, my swirling thoughts making me dizzy. A few deep breaths later, and I was calmer. There was nothing I could do with my knowledge, and it was better if I just put it out of my mind for now. I went back into the living room to see Carly was ready to go. She had her hair knotted back in a ponytail and her coat on.

"Leaving so soon?" I asked, puzzled at her hurry. She was usually the last up and ready to go.

"Yeah, get your coat on," she gestured impatiently, and I walked over to the closet to get my coat.

"Where are we going? Did you not hear Jules and her command not to go anywhere?"

"By yourself. She said by yourself. You're going with me. So it's fine." I shot her a sideways glance, but shrugged my jacket on, checking the pockets for my gloves. I had a feeling Jules wouldn't agree, seeing as how she thought Carly needed further self-defense training, but I also wasn't arguing the point. I had my phone and complete confidence in my own ability to protect myself.

"Where are we going?" I asked again, not forgetting she hadn't answered my question.

"The psychic."

Chapter Six

"It's freezing." I stamped my feet, feeling an overwhelming sense of déjà vu.

"Again, we're not leaving." Carly tossed a look over her shoulder at me, as she cupped her hands over the glass to stare into the shopfront. "He's coming in today, right?"

A flickering image of a young black man drifted through my mind, and I knew he would be here. "Yes, he's coming."

"Good. He's the last one in the phone book, and I want a complete report." She dropped down from standing on her tippy toes, satisfied with whatever she'd seen inside. "Typical setup. A desk in the front and then a *curtain* going to the back." There was no mistaking the derision when she said curtain. Carly thought the idea of fake psychics preying on innocent individuals was a crime. My thoughts about it were a little less decisive. I knew there was more to the world than what we could see. Hell, I was proof of it. Going after psychics hit a little too close to home for me.

"We could do our report on something else," I said a little desperately, trying to change her stubborn mind. "Do you really think it's a good idea to do our report on psychics, considering I am one? Kind of seems hypocritical to me, plus I'd rather not draw attention." The argument was a familiar one—one Carly ignored.

"Who better to expose a fraud than an actual psychic?" That was her standard argument, and I shook my head.

"But it's not proof, and I don't want to explain how we know they were fakes, or even why this was our topic." My hands were on my hips, and by this point, I didn't even feel the cold. "Why do you think Jake and Connor are having so many issues with the new captain? Huh? Because they're solving cases too easily, and they can't say they're using a psychic."

Carly appeared taken aback at my rant and asked, "Why are you so against this? We wouldn't be the first people to reveal a fake. They have TV shows about stuff like this."

"Because it's dangerous. For me. For Jake. And for every real psychic out there." I crossed my arms over my chest, done with my little tirade. It seemed like the more people that knew my secret, the more inclined I was to protect it.

"I'm sorry." She laid her hand on my arm, drawing my attention to her. "I didn't realize you felt so strongly." She shook her head. "I wasn't listening. We can change it if you want?"

Her offer was kind, but we didn't have enough time to change our report. I could see her willingness though, but we'd invested too much into this one to turn back now.

"I just don't want to be the circus act on display, you know?" I finally murmured. She frowned, then looped her arm in mine.

"Let's go get a coffee. This guy isn't here yet, and heck, we don't need him!" I could see what it cost her to give up the last psychic on her list. Carly wanted to mark everything off. Not interviewing the last one would leave our report incomplete in her mind, and drive her nuts.

"Let's not go crazy now. I mean, he is the last one in the phone book. Maybe we'll find the one real psychic in the yellow pages." We laughed, stepping into the warm shop, the smell of ground coffee beans hitting us. We ordered scones to go with the coffee and headed to a corner to sit and enjoy.

"You should take a chance with Danny." My words interrupted her taking a sip of coffee and she spilled some. "I … I'm not trying to meddle. Well, I guess actually I am. It's just, if you really like him, don't give up. He seems like a good guy, and I don't want you to miss out, because you're both too scared to go for it."

She didn't say anything, kind of just stared at me, so I rambled on.

"Not that I'm trying to tell you what to do, if I even could. It's just you're my friend, and I don't want you to feel that I would ever choose the group over you, because I wouldn't. I don't know, feel free to ignore me today. Apparently, I have all kinds of opinions." I glanced down at my scone. I'd crumbled it into pieces, while I was talking. I scooped up the crumbs and ate them anyway. They were really good scones.

"I'm glad." Her words drew my attention, but she's not looking at me. Instead, she's staring at her coffee like it holds the secrets to the universe. "It's stupid, but I've felt left out since senior year. So much happened that you didn't tell me about at the time. I shouldn't be so upset about it. You told me later, and you've never excluded me since then." She gave a one-shouldered shrug. "Danny feels like a kindred spirit. But I don't want to mess up the dynamic either. It finally feels like we have it together."

"We'll adapt. Nothing ventured, nothing gained," I smiled. "If you want that big, broody lug, then go for it."

She flicked a sugar packet at me.

"You're just jealous mine looks meaner than yours."

"Uh huh."

We finished our snack and headed out the door. Carly went to the left toward the car and I went to the right, back to the psychic.

"What ..."

"Where ..." We both spoke at once, and I figured it out. "Come on. We aren't leaving one psychic unaccounted for." A big smile covered Carly's face.

"Are you sure?"

"Hell yeah. Let's go."

When we got to the shop, the open sign was displayed, and a bell jingled when we yanked the door open. A deep voice called out a greeting and said they'd be with us in a minute. I took a second to look around the room. It was painted a cream color, naturalist photos hung on the walls, and a table with magazines was in the corner. Overall, not really what I expected for a 'fake' psychic. An attractive black man peeked through the beaded curtain a few minutes later.

"Can I help you?" He was pleasant, if puzzled. The door clearly stated readings by appointment only. I was actually surprised Carly hadn't called ahead to make an appointment. It was unlike her to miss something like that.

I couldn't help but notice he had an extremely deep voice; like James Earl Jones deep.

"Can you say, "Luke, I am your father?" I asked, completely serious, as Carly elbowed me. "Ow! What? You know you were thinking it."

A smile broke across his face, showcasing straight white teeth.

"You are the first to just out and out ask, though." He gazed up at the ceiling and frowned at me. "Luke, I am your father." He pitched it just right, the voice a low gravelly rumble. I clapped and said, "Nice!"

Carly tried to melt behind me, obviously embarrassed at my nerdy request. I dragged her out and asked, "Did you make an appointment?"

She shook her head no, "I didn't want him to prepare." I narrowed my eyes trying to puzzle that out.

"Prepare what?"

"Like, stuff." She waved an arm around, and I scanned the room, still confused by the concept of 'stuff.'

"Okaay," I replied distractedly, my attention captured by a drawing on the wall behind him. It was in the next room, and I hadn't seen it, because the curtain had hidden it from view. I walked toward it, brushing past him. The subject of the drawing drew me closer. It was a cabin, barely discernible from the growth surrounding it, abandoned and cast in shadows. There was something inherently disturbing about the drawing. It wasn't like the other pictures in the waiting room. This drawing had a presence, one that hinted at dark deeds and violent emotion.

"Who drew this?" I asked, already knowing it had been the gentlemen standing behind me.

"I did."

"Why?" He seemed to understand the deeper meaning in my question.

"A crime was committed there. A boy was murdered."

"How did you know?"

"I saw it." He paused as I studied the black and white sketch. There was no mistaking it was the same cabin Jake and I had found. "It was over a year ago, maybe two. I don't have visions often, but I kept picturing this place over and over. I finally decided to draw it, to get it out of my head."

"Did it work?" I asked, curious, wondering if drawing a vision would actually make it go away.

"No, it didn't, but one day, it was gone. Never pictured it again. I hung the sketch after that."

"Why hang it?" It was a dark piece, haunting to look at. The drawing had sent a chill down my spine when I'd seen it. It didn't seem like something you'd want around.

"To remember. That boy deserves to be remembered."

I nodded, understanding what he meant.

Carly decided at that moment to do her usual accusation.

"Are you a fake?" She pointed a finger at him, her head not even reaching the middle of his chest, a determined look on her face.

"No," I answered for him, already realizing he was the real deal.

"I ... what?" Carly asked, confused, as her attention turned to me.

"It looks like you found the only real psychic in the yellow pages, Carly." I told her, understanding dawning on his face, quickly followed by a pissed off expression.

"Perhaps you should leave." He held his arm up, pointing at the door.

"Wait!" Carly was catching on quick. "But if you're a real psychic, that means ..."

"You can go. I don't appreciate people coming into my shop with false agendas." He was adamant, even in the face of Carly's pleading expression. She wanted to discover more about him, and glancing around the room, I discovered more sketches. The idea they all might be visions, some possibly never resolved, had me walking closer.

"Nope. You too." He skewered me with a look. "There's something about you. Not sure what, but I'd rather not find out. So out."

"But ..." Carly protested, even as he kept a firm hand on her elbow, to escort her out. I took a last look at the sketches, turning to follow them.

"Wait." The voice hinted at age, but remained strong.

"Who are you, girl?"

The knowledge of what I was, the name her mind supplied me with rushed in.

"Addie," I replied, spinning around to look at her. "A truth seer?" It was a question, the term drawn from her mind, amongst a jumble of other possibilities when she asked. She appeared surprised, then shocked, as she considered my reply. Her face was darker than the guy in front of us. He was café au lait to her dark mocha. She studied me as intently, as I studied her. Her face was unlined, even though I knew she was in her eighties. She was gifted, the grandson in front of me inheriting her ability.

"Grannie …" he said, the warning clear in his voice.

"Wade, she doesn't know who she is." Her eyes narrowed on me. "And if she is what I think, then she's rare indeed."

The startling sound of a phone ringing interrupted my attempt to interpret what she meant.

"Oops, sorry!" Carly pulled her phone from her pocket, about to hit silent when she said, "It's Jake. Why is he calling?"

As soon as she asked, I reached into my pocket, realizing my phone was on silent, and Jake had been trying to reach me before going to Carly. He'd started with Jules, and I knew I'd be in for it the next time I saw her.

I held out my hand, and she gave me her phone.

"It was on silent," I answered him without even needing to hear the question.

"Okay. Massive heart attack averted. Where are you?" The residual fear thrumming though him hit me. He was at the docks, and desperately needed to know I was safe.

"I'm downtown in the antique district with Carly." I didn't bother to mention the psychic show going on in front of me.

"Stay there. I'll come get you," he muttered, his voice muffled, as he covered the phone to speak to someone.

"We can come to you." I wasn't ready to explain our location to him, and since I knew where he was, he didn't need to come to me. "We'll meet you at the docks."

He was distracted by someone near him. I could tell by how easily he agreed to my idea. "Okay. Be careful. And call Jules." The line went dead, and I sighed.

"We have to go," I told them, their gazes heavy on me.

"Don't forget to come back, child. You need to know who you are." Her words hinted at answers, and I nodded. The guy dropped his hand from Carly, and we turned to go.

The bell jingled as I paused at the door.

"The boy ... he got justice," I told him, watching as understanding crossed his face.

"Okay, that was unexpected." Carly clapped her hands together. "So where are we going?"

"The docks. They found a body."

When we arrived, there were officers swarming around. We parked a distance away and walked toward the caution tape. I'd texted Jake when we parked, and he said he'd come get us.

"Is it Deidre?" Carly's voice was hushed, not wanting to draw attention from the onlookers, cops and reporters hanging around like vultures.

"No." I shook my head. "It's the guy that kidnapped her." She turned stunned eyes to me, but Connor walked up then, grabbing my attention.

"This goes against protocol, but come on." He lifted the caution tape, and we slipped under. He walked a little way away from the gawking onlookers, giving me a pensive gaze. "A body was discovered in the river. We got the call, and when we arrived, we noticed the guy fit the description you gave of the kidnapper."

"It's him." I interrupted, glancing over his shoulder. I could see

Jake in the distance talking to a man. "Is that the new captain?" I asked, stretching to get a better look.

"Ah, yeah," he muttered, glancing over his own shoulder to be sure. "How did you know?"

"Carly asked if it was Deidre. I knew it wasn't, but I realized it was the guy that took her. It's kinda weird that he'd be dead, isn't it?"

"Yes, very odd. Which is why we wanted you to take a look, but then the new captain showed up." He frowned, his frustration evident. "Did you call Jules?"

I sighed, flicking a glance at him. "I texted her. No more phone on silent. I got the memo. You know, one day you'll slip and just say captain, not new captain."

"Maybe when he proves he's on our side." The words were muttered so low, I barely heard them. Their disillusionment with the prior captain, and now the barely restrained animosity for the new captain, worried me. I understood their reasons, but both of them had become more and more disgruntled by the way cases were handled. I was afraid if it continued, they would both wind up leaving the force.

The new captain walked away, and I could see Jake frowning after him. Not a good sign. I plucked at Connor's sleeve and started walking. Carly scurried behind us, reluctant to be left behind, but also disinclined to see a dead body.

"Seriously, guys, are we going to look at a dead body?"

"Yeah, would you rather stay back here?" Connor peered at her, but I already knew she wasn't getting left behind.

"No, I'm coming. I've never seen a dead body." Her curiosity was winning out over her natural aversion to seeing someone dead. The only dead bodies I'd ever seen had been in visions, and I shuddered at the memory of them. I had an idea of what I'd see when I got to Jake, but knowing never seemed to lessen the horror at the sight.

"Hey," he said as he immediately gripped me in a hug, kissing my forehead. "It's not pretty," he warned us, keeping me close as we stepped past more caution tape. The warning didn't quite come quick enough, as I saw the bloated body lying on the ground. The face staring up at me was distorted, but I recognized him. He was definitely the guy that had taken Deidre. I nodded, and Jake turned me away, using his body as a shield to the sight.

"Oh," Carly choked, looking at him. His skin had a grayish cast, his clothes were muddy, and his eyes were open and staring. "He drowned?"

"We think so. We'll need the coroner to tell us for sure."

"Yes," I replied as he finished, earning an inquisitive stare. "They threw him overboard."

"They?" His question brought to mind a scene of argument, men struggling, their faces in shadow as they fought. I shrugged, not seeing anything of use.

"Where or what did they throw him overboard from?" Connor's question elicited an easier answer, as I pointed to a similar boat cruising down the river in front of us.

"That. One like that."

"A tugboat."

We were interrupted then, as an angry voice asked, "What are you doing down here? This isn't the place for you."

I spun around, thinking the new captain had come back, but instead, saw Danny angrily looking at Carly, a towel draped around him. His jaw throbbed as he stood there tensely, waiting on an answer.

"I brought Addie! And what do you mean this isn't the place for me? And why are you all wet?" Carly's string of questions shed some light on the situation for me, and I glanced back down at our dead kidnapper.

"*You* fished him out of the river. And, Carly, he thinks you're too sweet to see death." I hummed to myself, sorting through the new information. Carly and Danny both flushed at my words.

"You think I'm sweet?" Her hand went to her hair, absentmindedly coiling a strand around her finger.

"Yes. You shouldn't have to see this." His embarrassed flush was oddly gratifying. It seemed the tough guy did possess softer emotions.

"You jumped in the river to pull him out?" My question was disbelieving as I scanned the wide swath of muddy river. From the shore, there was no mistaking the swirls and eddies hiding a strong current. Many had drowned in those waters, the dead man in front of me no exception.

"Wait … you jumped in the Mississippi River? Are you insane?" Carly screeched, and I determined he wasn't insane, but possibly suicidal, and definitely foolhardy. He had good intentions, but his track record of smart decisions was a little rocky. This was the same guy who had decided to turn on his drug dealers and testify. Jumping into a river with a dangerous current was on par for him. What worried me even more was the realization that he didn't think he deserved to live.

Connor had stepped away for a moment, while this was going on, but at his return, I could see more bad news was on the way.

"Guys," he said, getting our attention as we all turned to look at him. "Nash just called me. Another girl has been reported missing."

Chapter Seven

"Piper Henry was last seen leaving her Econ class yesterday morning. No one has seen or heard from her since. Her roommate thought it was unusual that she didn't come home last night, but didn't report it, until this morning, when she tried to call her and didn't get an answer." Connor rattled off the facts he'd been able to get from Nash as we all stood next to the shore of the Mississippi River. He scrutinized me and asked, "Did this guy kidnap her too?"

I nodded, knowing he had.

"So he kidnapped another girl and then got thrown off a tugboat all on the same day? Busy guy." Carly managed to sum it up and connect the dots all at one time.

"They're shipping them down the river in cargo containers," Jake muttered, shaking his head. He hadn't let go of me, and I was grateful for his support. The pieces were clicking together, and I remembered being threatened myself with being sold.

"They're trafficking." My words had all of them stilling, the idea of human trafficking going on in our small town, the girls being taken from our local college horrifying each of us.

"Cargo containers aren't warm." Danny's observation had us looking at him. "I'm just saying. I've been inside of a few, welding. They're damn cold, especially now. And you said Deidre was warm. So she's not in a cargo container." He jerked his shoulder, uncomfortable at the attention, but I also noticed he hovered next to Carly; close, but not touching. I hoped the lack of touching had more to do with him being soaking wet, and not because he didn't want to touch her.

"Which reminds me, you need to change. You're gonna freeze." Danny glanced down, seeming surprised by his own soaked state.

"Oh my God, she's right. You have to get out of those wet clothes." Carly gasped, plucking at the wet material that clung to his well-defined chest. "Not that I mind the view, but I don't want you to get pneumonia or something."

He gave her a startled look, and then a pleased smirk replaced it. Jake attempted to cover a knowing smirk with his hand, but Connor didn't even bother, a wide grin splitting his face.

"I mean I appreciate the view as well, but we can't have you getting sick now, sweetie," Connor said in a false soprano, wiggling his fingers at Danny, who swung a punch that Connor deftly dodged. "Getting slow, must be the cold, right?"

We all laughed, none of us forgetting the dead man at our feet, but relieved to have something else to focus on. Our dead kidnapper had taken his knowledge to the grave with him, but he still might have some secrets I could learn.

"They're right, man," Jake interrupted. "You need to change. It's freezing out here. I mean your nipples are practically headlights." The stunned silence only lasted a second before we were all laughing, and Danny was crossing his arms to hide the 'headlights.' It wasn't often Jake joined in the teasing, usually keeping to his role as the serious one, but when he did, it was all the more hilarious.

"Fuck y'all," Danny told us, flipping the bird, but his smile belied any insult.

"We need to finish clearing the scene. Regroup at our place tonight?" Jake still had his arm wrapped around me as he said it, and as everyone nodded, it didn't escape me he'd referred to his apartment as 'our place.' I wasn't sure how I felt about it, but the dead man in front of me demanded that more important matters take precedence.

Jake dropped a quick kiss on my cheek, whispering, "I love you." I gave him a tight squeeze around his middle, echoing his words.

As we walked back toward the caution tape, I heard Carly ask Danny, "Do you want a ride to your apartment?"

"I've got my bike," he replied, and I heard the distinct pause as Carly replied disbelievingly, "You want to ride your bike while you're soaking wet?"

"Uh," was his intelligent response, and I smiled as Carly said, "Nope. Not happening. I'll take you home, you change, and then bring you back for your bike. You'll be there tonight?"

"Yes," he answered, and I imagined he didn't know what had just happened. Carly tended to have that effect on people when she was on a roll. I opened the door to the backseat, already knowing he was coming. The drive to his apartment was quick, since he lived only a few blocks from the river. Some of the neighborhoods around here had started to be revitalized, people buying the old homes and making them showplaces. There was a push to develop the abandoned warehouses and turn them into high end condos, bars, restaurants and hotels. The idea was good, but there were still plenty of rundown apartment complexes around, and one of them was Danny's. We parked, and I thought he'd just run in and change, but that wasn't the case.

"Come on," he said, leaning back into the car. "It's not safe for you to stay down here." Carly turned the car off and hopped out. I followed more slowly, looking around. The area was rundown and old. It had the feeling of being tired, more than criminal. I thought Danny was being a tad overprotective, but I should be used to that by now. I was surrounded by overprotective peeps.

73

The reason for Carly's eagerness was apparent, the second we stepped into his apartment. She should be dizzy with the way her head kept turning to look at everything. The place was clean. I'd give him that. Old as dirt, no way to hide it, but he didn't have stuff lying around, and it smelled clean. I wasn't sure if I was expecting the odor of sweat, or maybe joints. I really couldn't be sure with Danny. The kitchen counters were an old wood grain laminate, and I thought the carpet might have been orange at one point, but it was hard to tell with the stains. There was an old plaid couch and some folding chairs to sit on, so I sat on the couch.

I was exhausted, the day full of unforeseen surprises, and the knowledge of another missing girl was tough for me to accept. It felt like I should have done more to prevent it. If I'd asked more questions, maybe we would have found the kidnapper before he wound up in the Mississippi.

I hadn't forgotten my startling meeting with Wade and his Grannie, either. The thought that they may have answers for me wouldn't leave me alone. I'd never met anyone with abilities, much less someone who seemed to know what I was. It had never occurred to me that what I could do had a name.

Truth seeker. The term drifted through my mind, along with something else she'd thought … *human lie detector*.

The idea was appropriate enough. My ability could easily be seen as one that could detect lies. It didn't matter what people told me. I could see the truth when they asked a question. My eyes felt weighted, as thoughts continued tumbling around inside of my head: the image of the kidnapper's bloated body, Grannie's face, Piper, and Deidre's disappearance, combined with the knowledge that if we didn't find the girls quickly, they would be gone forever.

I jerked awake, not recognizing where I was, a low murmur of voices grabbing my attention. My heart raced from a combination of the dream I'd just had and confusion over where I was. The thumping slowed as I remembered Carly and I had gone with Danny to his apartment. My fingers ran over the rough plaid material on the couch, and I recognized Carly's voice. The dream was slipping away from me, and I closed my eyes tightly, trying to recall the details of it. The dream had consisted of flashes from the numerous questions I'd heard, but something had struck me, a flicker of an image that I didn't think was the past, but the future. If I could only grab on to it.

A cry escaped me, as I finally had it, and Carly rushed over to me.

"Hey, are you okay?" she asked, hugging me. "We saw you fall asleep and figured you needed the rest. Did you have a bad dream?"

I held tightly to her, my fear for her overwhelming. Danny caught my eyes over her shoulder, and from his expression he realized whatever I'd seen was disturbing.

"It's okay," she soothed, rocking me. "It was just a bad dream." I nodded and loosened my hold, not wanting to frighten her. I forced a smile and stood up.

"We should go drop Danny off and get over to Jake's." My voice was surprisingly steady as I said it, and Carly agreed, grabbing her purse.

We walked out of the apartment, Carly moving ahead, as Danny clutched my arm. His grip was tight enough to stop me, but not painful.

"Is it Carly?" His words slammed into me with the force of a freight train, and I swayed, seeing the possibilities more clearly than ever. He held me up, and I heard the fear in his voice when he said, "I guess that's my answer."

"We have to protect her." I groped behind me blindly, catching his hand in mine and squeezing hard. "We have to." I felt more than saw his nod in the dark hallway and released him. My legs were shaky as I walked down the hall hearing Carly call behind her, "Come on, slowpokes. We'll be late."

We dropped Danny back off at the docks with the promise that we would go straight to Jake's place, no stopping anywhere. Carly kept her word, and we arrived in no time. She stopped me as I was getting out of the car.

"Are you okay?" Her eyes were concerned, and I could feel the worry in her question. I nodded, attempting to be positive. She didn't look fooled. "It's been a crazy day. When you fell asleep on the couch, I convinced Danny to let you sleep for a few minutes. I thought it would do you good, but you seem out of sorts since you woke up. Did you have one of *those* dreams?"

I knew what she meant—did I have one of my psychic dreams—and as much as it pained me to do it, I lied to her.

"No," I said, shaking my head. "It's just, everything from the last few days caught up with me at once." I forced a smile, wondering if I was making a mistake not telling her what I'd seen. "But with the missing girl, it got me thinking." I paused, catching her eye. "We need to do another self-defense class with the guys." I could see her about to protest the idea, so I added, "With Danny, we have sparring partners for everyone." That stopped her protest in its tracks. I knew she'd take any opportunity she could to see Danny hot and sweaty.

"You know that sounds like an excellent idea," she nodded, her grin telling me she'd figured out the potential advantages of sparring with Danny. I laughed and told her, "Get your mind out of the gutter."

A low rumble interrupted her reply, as a big motorcycle came up alongside her car. Danny removed his helmet and nodded, "Ladies."

We got out of the car and waited on the sidewalk for him to join us. Carly not so subtly checked his ass out as he bent over to store the helmet. I poked her in the side, and she shrugged, mouthing, "What?"

"Do I want to know?" He stepped between us, catching the tail end of our little mime show. Carly immediately flushed at the thought of being caught ogling him, and I laughed.

"Doubt it." I answered, smirking at Carly's flush. He nodded, a faint smile playing on his full lips.

As soon as we stepped inside the apartment, I was once again engulfed in a bone crushing hug. "What were you thinking?! Do you know how worried I was?"

The force of her emotions almost had my knees buckling as I felt them wash over me with her screeched questions. She seemed to realize it the second it happened, because I heard, "I'm sorry. Damn it. I know better. I was worried and angry."

I managed a chuckle as I told her, "I noticed."

"Jules, could you quit trying to break my girlfriend?" Jake sighed, pulling me into his embrace.

"Uh huh, and who was the one calling me in a panic earlier today because you couldn't get a hold of her? Huh? Oh yeah, that was you, buddy!" She poked him in the chest with her finger, and went to sit on the loveseat. I blinked, surprised at her little outburst. She was definitely not herself as she sat there frowning. Connor looked a little puzzled too as he went and tucked an arm around her. I curled up on Jake's lap as Danny and Carly sat on the sofa, a little closer than normal, I noted happily.

"So obviously, we know another girl is missing; the kidnapper is dead; it's definitely a trafficking ring; and since our dead guy is tied to the girls, maybe we can get a little more info on the missing girls." Jake summarized the events of the day, going over the identity of the kidnapper, Tyler Hamilton, and what we knew of the girls. "Anything else we need to add?" he finished, and Carly raised a questioning eyebrow to me, while Danny gave me a hard look. I knew Carly wanted to know if I was going to mention meeting the psychic earlier, but I wasn't ready. This wasn't the time or place. They might be able to answer questions about who I was, but we needed to focus on the missing girls.

Danny was a little harder to ignore. He suspected Carly was in danger, and I knew it. I gave a slight shake of my head in the negative, and his eyes narrowed. I wondered if he would push it, but he sat back, draping his arm over the back of the couch, not quite putting his arm around Carly. Her head turned and she wiggled a bit, looking confused by the sudden turnabout in Danny's attitude. He stared at me, stating his position. If I wouldn't protect her, he would. I frowned, not liking his implication. If I thought telling everyone right now, including Carly, what I saw would help, I would do it in a second, but I didn't believe that. It would only put everyone more on edge, and resolve nothing.

"We're having dinner at Mom's house tomorrow," Jules threw in, redirecting our attention to her.

"Okay," Jake drawled, obviously puzzled by her telling everyone. He glanced over at Carly and Danny. They'd never been to his Mom's for dinner, and none of us sure if Jules' invitation included them.

"Them too," she added, catching our looks. "The whole freaking world is invited to the baby party." She stood up and left the room with that proclamation.

Jake shut his eyes, a pained expression on his face. He kissed my temple and shifted me, standing up. "I'll be back in a minute." Connor had stood up to follow Jules, but Jake waved him back. "Let me." He gave him an understanding nod, but Connor just looked confused.

"I think Natalie and John are expecting baby number two," I told them. Connor sat back down, but still glanced at the door Jules had disappeared through every few seconds. He knew he was missing something, but until Jules told him, there was nothing I could do.

"The Kincaid's are really nice," I told the other two as they sat there uncomfortably.

"Oh well, I wouldn't want to impose," Carly started, obviously feeling like the invite was lacking.

"No, no. You need to come. Both of you. You'll be expected." Connor shot me a 'what are you doing?' look, and I quirked an eyebrow, asking him to play along. Jules' invitation for the family dinner had sparked an idea, and I needed them to attend.

"Yeah, if Jules mentioned it to her parents they'll be expecting you and you don't want to disappoint them." Connor backed me, having no idea what I was planning, but trusting me. Danny had refusal written across his face, but then Carly turned to him.

"You'll go, right? I'd hate to be a fifth wheel." I almost chuckled at the change in his expression. He did a complete about-face, nodding as she spoke.

"If you'll be there, I'll be there," he told her, causing Connor to blink and look at me. He jerked his head to the door, cutting his eyes and basically trying to tell me to get up and go to the door with him. I pretended like I didn't see him, and he frowned.

"Addie," he called me out, and I glared at him. "What's the deal?" His question was pointed, and I stood up.

"We'll be right back," I tossed over my shoulder, stepping in front of Connor as we got to the door.

"Are we in the fucking Twilight Zone?" he hissed, as soon as we were in the hallway. "Jules …" he waved an arm down the hall, not even knowing how to describe her outburst. "And Danny and Carly? Did I miss that? Oh, and don't think I missed those looks between you and Danny, and you and Carly. What is going on?" His frustration hit me in a wave, and I leaned against the wall, sorting through everything, deciding to answer the simplest things first.

"Yes, Carly has a huge crush on Danny, and I think he might return it. I don't know about Jules. Thanks for going along. I wanted Danny and Carly at the dinner tomorrow."

That effectively deflected his line of questioning and gave me breathing room. "Yeah, why did you want them there?"

"I saw something this afternoon—the reason Danny was willing to jump in the river to pull the dead guy out. He doesn't have a reason to live. He thinks it doesn't matter if he dies."

Connor's eyebrows drew down at my words, and he appeared horrified. "What?" I nodded, remembering the swirl of thoughts Carly's question had set loose.

"I was thinking we could invite Danny's parents to the dinner tomorrow." I gave him a wide-eyed stare, and he caught on immediately.

"Force a reunion."

"Mmhmm. They miss him, and he hasn't budged on a reconciliation, but maybe if he saw them … listened to them."

"He'd forgive himself for Samuel," Connor said, nodding. "Not a bad idea. Granted, it could also blow up in your face. You do realize that?"

"Yes, but I have a good feeling."

Jules and Jake came down the hall then, and Connor leaned down and whispered, "Don't think I forgot my other questions." He gave me a narrow glance and turned to greet Jules.

"Hey, babe." He wrapped her in a big hug, not asking questions, and she smiled at him as they walked back into the living room.

Jake stared at me knowingly and then asked, "Do you know?" I nodded, his question confirming what I'd learned from Carly's question earlier that morning. It seemed like a lifetime ago now. I hugged him, knowing he hurt for Jules.

"It's hard for her. John doesn't know, neither does Natalie." I peeked up at him, a question in my eyes. He nodded. "She was okay with you knowing, and I told her Connor needed to know. He'll understand, but she's understandably nervous about telling him." I leaned my head on his chest, hugging him tighter. Jules and Jake were extremely close, barely a year apart and best friends. They felt each other's pain like their own, and would do anything for one another. But neither could fix this, and it hurt.

"So what were you and Connor whispering about?" Jake asked, looking down at me, an expectant look on his face. I grinned, using him as leverage as I rocked back. He braced himself, his arms locked behind me as I hung suspended.

"Our torrid affair that we don't want anyone to find out about." I managed to keep a straight face as I said it, causing him to loosen his arms a tiny bit, so I had the sensation of falling before he locked them back, and kept me upright. I laughed and he said, "The truth."

81

"I want Danny and Carly at the family dinner tomorrow." He cocked his head, waiting. "And I want you to invite Danny's parents," I finished in a rush, watching his eyes widen the slightest bit. He glanced toward the living room and then back at me. "You have your reasons?" I nodded, glancing over my shoulder and catching a glimpse of the back of Danny's head. He was teetering on the edge, and we had to find a way to push him back.

"I know we normally wouldn't meddle like this, but it's important." My arms were still wrapped around his waist, and he tugged me toward him, holding me tight.

"Okay, I'll make sure they're there." He didn't ask any other questions, trusting me. I burrowed my head against his chest, his cotton scent comforting me. This day ranked high on the list for number of revelations in one day. Most of them had been challenging and upsetting, leaving me wondering what tomorrow would bring.

Chapter Eight

"How bad is this gonna be?" Connor whispered, leaning down and blocking anyone's view of me. I winced, seeing a vague flicker of shouting and Danny storming out. Predicting the future wasn't something I did normally, but in certain circumstances, such as a person's gut reaction, it was easy to guess what could happen.

"Fantastic," he muttered, straightening up.

"Maybe you should unhook the battery on his bike or something? So he can't get away?" I suggested hopefully. Connor gave me a disgusted look.

"You don't mess with a man's bike, woman."

I rolled my eyes and hissed, "Then you stand in front of the door when he decides to storm out." That idea had him squirming uncomfortably. Danny had no compunction about decking a man, even if he was a cop.

We'd all arrived at Jake's parents a little early. His momma's warm hug as familiar to me as my own mom's, but I could tell it had caught Danny off guard. Natalie and John had made their announcement of the newest Kincaid almost immediately, too excited to wait any longer.

Connor and I were standing next to the front window, keeping a lookout for the Phillips, while Jake and Danny talked about the docks where Danny worked. Considering where the kidnapper had been spotted in the water, there was a good chance something was happening at the docks where Danny worked. It was a massive complex, and Jake wanted inside information about the inner workings.

I tugged on Connor's sleeve, seeing a car turn into the driveway. He glanced out and then over at Jake, with a small nod indicating it was show time. We all had our fingers crossed that being around friends and in neutral territory might smooth their reunion, but I was aware of the dark emotions that consumed Danny. The guilt, regret, and anger hadn't abated in the last year, but only grew as it directed itself inward, destroying his ability to heal. I could only hope this had the effect I wanted and didn't spin him completely out of control.

The ring of the doorbell surprised a few of them, not realizing we were waiting on two more for dinner. Jake's dad answered the door, greeting Mr. and Mrs. Phillips warmly. I had my eyes on Danny though, watching his expression as he caught sight of them. There was pain and longing before he closed himself off, but it was enough for me.

"Daniel!" Mrs. Phillips cried out, tears filling her eyes. It was the first time she'd seen him in over two years. She rushed to him, throwing her arms around him. He didn't reciprocate, and she slowly backed away, taking in every nuance of him as he stood there uncomfortably. His gaze flickered to her and then his father and he looked away, unable to make eye contact with them.

"We've missed you, Daniel. So very, very much." Her words were a whisper, but we all heard them, the room still as we watched their reunion.

"Son," his father said, a hand outstretched. This snapped Danny out of the frozen state he was in, and with a snarl he stepped around his mother, careful not to hit her, but there was no mistaking his anger.

"I don't deserve that word," he gritted out, headed straight for the door. Connor made a step toward it to block him from leaving, but I slid in front of it first. It was the first time I'd seen Danny so angry, and it was truly frightening. Every part of him was drawn tight, from the clenched fists hanging next to him, to his black stare, ice cold and intimidating, but I was ninety percent sure he wouldn't hit me. *Maybe seventy*, I amended, as he leaned down and growled, "Move, or I will go through you."

"No," I told him, standing firm. Jake and Connor were on either side of him, ready to grab him if he swung at me. Carly hovered behind them, a pained expression on her face. His parents watched us, defeat warring with sorrow in their expressions.

He rocked back, echoing me, "No?"

He couldn't believe I was standing up to him, and part of him wanted me too, firming my resolve.

"NO."

His eyes narrowed, and he moved toward me, his hands on my waist to set me aside. I could see Jake and Connor stepping forward, and shook my head at them. I stared straight into Danny's eyes, and told him the words he refused to believe.

"You deserve to live." He shook his head violently, and I could feel his fingers pressing into my side.

"No, I don't," he gritted out between clenched teeth, the muscle working in his jaw as he attempted to control himself. "You need to move."

"You need to listen to them." He shook his head as I nodded mine. "Yes, you owe them that much."

His head reared back, and he blinked at me.

"You heard me. You owe them a conversation. You're the reason Samuel was taken. You've blamed yourself for what's happened for too long. You should at least have the courtesy to let them tell you how they feel." I saw the slight shake of his head, and the sudden fear in his eyes. He didn't want to hear their accusations, or feel their pain on top of his own.

Connor's eyes widened at my words, no doubt wondering what I was playing at. I knew Danny would keep running, avoiding what he believed he'd caused, and never find any peace. He would wind up dead by his own hand, unable to escape the demons he'd created.

I needed him to hear his parents, so maybe they could give him the forgiveness he couldn't give himself.

"Are you going to deny them that? After everything?" I glared at him, forcing myself to be angry, so he would listen to me. "Are you a coward, as well?"

"You have no idea what you're talking about!" he roared, rage causing him to push me against the door, his fingers digging deep into my sides, leaving bruises.

"Then tell me!" I screamed back, remembering the emotions I'd sensed swirling deep inside of him every time a question was brought up about Samuel or his parents. "Tell me how you decided to narc on your supplier, because Sam thought it was the right thing to do. Tell me how you made the decision to walk away from it all, because Sam asked you to." His eyes grew damp as I pushed, telling him what I'd seen. "Tell me how you blame yourself for his death every single day. Tell me about the guilt, the regret, and the sheer hatred you feel toward yourself every single day. Tell me. And then tell them." I pointed to his parents, and his head turned, his eyes closing at the sight of his mother's tears.

"Look at me!" I shouted, and his gaze shot back to mine as everyone else jumped. "Now, let me tell you how they feel." He shook his head desperately, but I pushed. "Let me tell you how your mother cries herself to sleep at night, because she lost two sons instead of one. How your dad blames himself, because he was late picking Sam up. How your mom almost took the entire bottle of prescription pills the doctor gave her, because she can't bear knowing you blame yourself."

"Wha …" He looked so lost standing there as I told him the things I'd seen countless times, when Jake talked to his parents.

"Maybe you should let them tell you how they feel. So at least they know they tried," I whispered to him, feeling the weight of him against me as he sagged. He wasn't digging into me anymore, so much as I was holding him up. I wrapped an arm around him, leading him, and he let me, too stunned by my revelations to protest. We walked to the couch, and I pushed him down.

"Are you going to listen now?" He nodded absently, still lost in what I'd revealed, and I looked over at his parents.

"I'm sorry. I shouldn't have told everyone your business." They shook their heads, not seeming to care, but I still felt guilty. I was the keeper of others' secrets, and I didn't take the job lightly. They sat on either side of Danny, and his mom hesitantly took his hand, smiling as he allowed it.

The rest of us backed out of the room, giving them the privacy they needed. I didn't feel like Danny would run, but I locked the front door, just in case. Jake saw me and smiled as he settled his head on top of mine.

"You okay?" He'd been worried and was pissed at Danny touching me, but trusted I knew what I'd been doing. I spoke instead of nodding, not wanting him to move his head from mine.

"Yeah, I'll warn you now, there might be bruises." I felt him tense up at my words and squeezed him extra tight. "I might bruise, but I don't break. He needed someone to get in his face. I thought I had the best chance of not getting punched." He growled at that thought, making me chuckle.

"You laugh, but it would have been a fight if he'd tried."

"I know," I told him, relieved it hadn't come to that. Danny truly was a good guy, but the demons that haunted him were fierce and made him dangerous in many respects.

"Why do you always have to be the one placing yourself in danger?" His question was rhetorical, but I could see the reasoning. I often knew where the danger was, and felt like I could step into a dangerous situation, already having an escape plan ready. When I told him this, he closed his eyes.

"That's not comforting at all. Just so you know."

After we had dinner, which was only marginally awkward after everything that had gone down, I had Jake drop me off at my mom's. She'd gotten a new car, and I could finally have mine back again.

"I'm gonna go into the precinct. See what I can dig up. At least the dead kidnapper is our case." I heard the irritation in his voice as he continued. "Maybe if I can find some evidence linking him to the kidnapped girls, we can get the case moving in the right direction."

"He had to transport them somehow. The easiest way would be a car. Did the girls have cars?" I wasn't sure if the kidnapper had taken the girls in their own cars or if he'd had a car. If we could find the vehicle, maybe there was evidence linking the two cases.

"No, they didn't." I heard his excitement as he made the same connections I did. "I can't believe we missed that."

"Well, it wasn't your case," I murmured, and he gave me a faint smile.

"Where is the kidnapper's car?" he asked, knowing this would be an easy question for me. I rattled off an address, and puzzlement crossed his face for a second, then it cleared and he said, "That's the dock."

I remembered the enormous parking lot Carly and I had driven through, to get to Jake and the dead body yesterday, and knew it would be a needle in a haystack to find.

"What type of car was he driving?" I told him a black Chevy Cobalt and he nodded. It narrowed it down, but would still take a little time to find. If our kidnapper was working with other people, and we were positive he was, they could have already disposed of the evidence. Jake leaned over and kissed me. His gentle kiss turned fiercely possessive as I tugged on the hair at the nape of his neck. I wanted him closer, and he obliged, tightening his arm around me as we leaned closer to one another. I bit his lower lip and soothed it with a kiss, our lips meeting over and over again, as neither of us attempted to pull away. I pressed kisses against the skin of his jaw, catching the faintest whiff of his aftershave, the scent sending spirals of lust through me. I kissed him harder, my lips finding the curve of his upper lip and nuzzling it.

"I have to call Connor," he muttered, his hands under my shirt as his thumb caressed the side where Danny had bruised me. My laugh was muffled as I kissed him more firmly.

"Always Connor interrupting us," I said, pulling my mouth from his as his hand slid out from under my shirt and rested on my ass. He gave a light squeeze and I yelped, surprised by his action.

"We have to find that car," he said, his reluctance at letting me go obvious. I nodded, knowing he was right. He glanced toward the front door. "Are you going to be okay? I don't like the idea of you going home alone."

"I'll be fine," I told him, kissing him quickly on the corner of his mouth before jumping out of the car. I knew if I let him think too long on it, he'd call Jules to bring me home. "Be careful."

"You too." He gave me a serious look, and I nodded obediently. I really had no desire to be kidnapped or to hear any more questions about the kidnapped girls. "Tell your mom and grandfather I said hello."

I smiled, knowing he liked hanging out with my grandfather. "I will." I slammed the door shut on his black Camaro, a leftover from his undercover drug days, and watched him drive away.

I bounced inside. The door was unlocked, because neither of them remembered to lock it during the day. My grandfather was always there, so that somehow made it okay to leave the door unlocked.

"Hello! Anyone home? I'm here to rob the place."

"Thank goodness. I've been wanting a bigger television," my mom said as she walked from the kitchen and gave me a big hug. I hugged her back, forever grateful for her. I'd had a peek at just how much she loved me when I'd been shot, and it was difficult to describe the level of emotions I'd felt in those moments. Suffice to say, my mother was the constant in my life, and I couldn't imagine life without her.

"Where's Paw Paw?" I asked, figuring he was watching a Nascar race.

"Watching a race, where else?" she replied, walking back to the kitchen. "I've got cookies. You want some?"

"Is the Pope Catholic?" I answered, following her. Paw Paw had come to live with us after my grandmother's death, at my insistence. He was one of my favorite people, and I missed seeing him every day. Mom and I talked on the phone constantly, but Paw Paw was deaf as a doorknob, so he wouldn't talk on the phone. I made it a point to come by at least once a week to see him, though.

"Is Jake working on the case for those missing girls? It's terrible. One might have run away, but now there's two. That sounds suspicious to me. You need to be careful, you hear?" She pointed the spatula at me as she took the cookies off the pan, and I nodded, having heard it all before. I knew where the concern came from, tempering my aggravation. "And now I heard they found a

90

man in the Mississippi River, drowned. What is the world coming to?"

She turned back to the cookies, but her question had opened the door in my mind. There was no answer, but the darkness consumed me as I balanced on the edge of the door in my mind. The dizziness that accompanied the absence of everything caused me to stumble forward into it.

"ADDIE!" Her voice screamed at me pulling me from the darkness, a blackness that I now realized was filled with images, blinks in time, rushing by so fast, it only appeared to be an empty vortex.

I blinked up at her, and she clutched me to her. "You fell off the barstool, your eyes just blank and staring. I thought you were having a stroke!" She scanned me. "Did you have a stroke? Oh my God, do I need to take you to the hospital?"

I shook my head, knowing I hadn't had a stroke, but relieved she'd been able to snap me out of the darkness.

"What is going on?" Paw Paw asked, shuffling into the kitchen. "I heard you shouting."

"Wow, you must have been loud if Paw Paw heard you," I muttered, and Mom laughed semi-hysterically.

"It's alright," she told him, and he cupped a hand around his ear. "IT'S ALRIGHT," she shouted loudly, and he jumped saying, "You don't have to shout." She peered up at me, exasperated, and I laughed, familiar with the fine line between loud enough for him to hear and shouting.

"We have cookies," I told him loudly, and he nodded, grinning. I pulled myself up from the floor and helped Mom up.

"Maybe you should go to the doctor," Mom suggested as we ate our cookies. Paw Paw had left to finish watching the race, and I shook my head. "No, I'm fine. It was a weird thing. Probably low

91

blood sugar." She gave me a disbelieving look, but stopped pushing for the moment. I knew she was only gearing up to launch another attack when I wasn't expecting it.

"Do you have plans for Mardi Gras?" she asked, changing the subject. I shook my head, having forgotten Mardi Gras was coming up in another week. "Classes are out Monday and Tuesday, right?"

"Yeah, that'll be nice," I said, excited at the prospect. College was better than high school in a lot of ways, but it was still school, which I despised. She nodded knowingly, already aware of my dislike for the educational institution. It wasn't the learning that bothered me, as much as the feeling of being trapped by school and homework. Homework alone was reason enough for me not to like going.

"They're supposed to have a parade downtown on Monday," she mentioned, and I gave her a funny look. Neither of us were parade people. She shrugged and said, "Thought I'd mention it. But maybe you should see about making a doctor's appointment, while you're off. You know, just a checkup." I rolled my eyes, laughing.

"I should have known." I gave her a kiss on the cheek and hopped down from the barstool. "I have to go. I've got an early class and some studying to do. Thanks for giving my car back."

"You're welcome. Thanks for letting me borrow it," she replied drily.

"What's mine is yours!" I told her with a salute, as I headed out. "Bye, Paw Paw!" I shouted into the living room, and he waved at me.

I got in my car and had to sit there for a second, remembering where everything was. People had been chauffeuring me for so long, I'd almost forgotten how to drive. I put it in gear and headed to the dorms, flicking on my headlights when someone flashed theirs at me. "Oops," I whispered to myself, knowing I'd 'forget' to mention that to my mom. I was notorious for driving without headlights, always forgetting to turn them on when it got dark.

When I got to the dorm, I had to park a few rows from the entrance, because it was late. I huddled into my jacket, hurrying toward the door. I wasn't paying attention, as I took the stairs two at a time, eager to get out of the icy wind. I slammed into what felt like a brick wall, but clearly it wasn't, as it grasped me by the arms and muttered, "What the hell are you doing? Does Jake know you're by yourself? What if I'd been a kidnapper?"

His questions came at me hard and furious, but my training kicked in equally as quickly. I twisted hard, going limp and forcing him to readjust his grip. I used the moment to stomp down on his foot and slip out of his grasp. He was stunned, more by my quick action than by any pain in his foot. Steel-toed boots tended to do a good job of protecting a man's feet.

"IF you'd been a kidnapper, that is what I would have done, plus screamed really loudly. But since you weren't, I figured I'd save us the scene. And yes, Jake knows I'm by myself. It's not supposed to be dangerous walking from my car to my dorm." He stared at me, and I shrugged, raising my hands up. "Not supposed to be. Also, quit throwing that many questions at me at once. I don't like it. And what are *you* doing here?"

He was uncomfortable with my question, and as we were still standing outside in the cold, and I was freezing, I tugged him inside. "Well?"

"I wanted to …" He paused and I waited, wondering what the hell was going on. Danny had never been to my dorm, ever, and standing here looking at me awkwardly was the last thing I ever expected to see. "Apologize." Alright, actually that was the last thing I ever expected.

"Hang on, I think I need to sit down," I replied with a smirk, and he gave me a semi-glare.

"I'm serious," he bit out, looking a tad grumpy and extremely uncomfortable at being here apologizing.

"Yeah, I see that. Come on." I waved him toward the stairs. My dorm apartment was on the second floor, and I used the stairs as my rationale that I worked out every day.

Once we were settled, mugs of coffee in hand, he said, "I would not have pegged you for a chicory girl. Too dark and bitter."

"Yeah, I get that a lot. Acquired taste from my grandfather," I replied, sitting back in my little chair. Danny was on the couch, mainly because I was afraid his sheer mass would break any of my other furniture. It wasn't exactly good quality to start with. All of it either came from a box or was collected from the thrift store.

"I wanted to apologize for earlier today. One, I shouldn't have come at you like that. And two, I hurt you, and I'm truly sorry about that." His sincerity shone through with each word, and I appreciated his apology, even though I didn't feel the need for it. When I told him that, he shook his head.

"Danny, have you ever cornered a wild animal?"

"No, that'd be stupid and dangerous," he answered, giving me a confused look.

"Exactly. It is stupid and dangerous. And today you were the wild animal. I knew that, and I took a risk, because you deserve to be happy. A lot of bad shit happened, Danny, and it's easy to blame yourself, but the truth is, the people who are truly to blame are in prison right now. Don't lock yourself away too, okay?" I smiled at him. "I know a few people that would miss you."

He gave me a reluctant grin, and took a sip of coffee, his mouth twisting at the bitter taste. "Okay, I usually take my coffee black, but this is a bit much." He went to the fridge and removed the creamer, pouring it in liberally. He raised an eyebrow at me, daring me to comment, and I just shook my head.

"That's not the only reason you stopped by?" I inquired, sipping my own dark brew, sans creamer, but filled with sugar, a fact I didn't plan to admit.

"No," he took a sip and seemed to like the taste a bit better with creamer. "What did you see earlier this afternoon? It was something about Carly, wasn't it?" His questions didn't bother me, only causing the same image I'd seen in my dream to come back.

"Why do you ask? I wouldn't have thought you would be so concerned about Carly." I admitted to myself I was fishing for information. Carly was damn near an open book when it came to Danny, but he'd managed to keep his feelings where she was concerned hidden from me, and I wanted to make sure she wasn't about to get hurt.

He sat back against the couch and the springs groaned, causing him to look down. "Am I gonna wind up on the floor?" I shrugged, uncertain if he would or not. He shook it off and said, "Talking about how I feel doesn't come naturally to me. Never has. Hell, I don't know if I could explain it right if I tried. So I'm not going to." He gave me a pointed look and asked, "How do I feel about Carly?"

The emotions rushed through me, all good, and I smiled, blinking back stupid tears. He was protective of her, of course. No way around that with these guys, but she made him happy, a feeling he had forgotten. She was too good for him. He knew that without a shadow of a doubt, but the sense they were kindred spirits filled him. A feeling Carly had as well. He was terrified of hurting another person he loved, the fear keeping him from pursuing her, but he wanted to try. He wanted to be good enough for her.

"You are good enough for her," I murmured, clearing my throat. He nodded, tense and uncomfortable with the thought of giving me carte blanche into his emotions for her.

"You see way more than I realize, don't you?" I smiled at what he thought I was capable of. He'd started to understand how strong my ability was that first night, but it was all vague. He didn't quite understand how I experienced the feelings, as well as saw the truth.

"It's unusual for me to have a truly psychic vision; one of the future. My gift is more one of sorting through fact versus fiction. Seeing the truth amongst the lies. I know facts, things that have happened, even if there's no way I should be able to know them. It's always been a subtle gift." I paused, taking a deep breath. "Carly … I had a flash of her, blood running down her face, as if she'd been hit. I don't know how or when it'll happen, or even if it will. The future changes with every decision we make. Telling you now may be enough to keep it from ever happening."

"But you don't believe that." He didn't bother to phrase it as a question, but I nodded anyway. "If I ask you questions, could we discover more about it?"

I shrugged, uncertain, since trying to question the future was like walking through sand that was constantly shifting.

He leaned toward me, his face fierce, and asked, "Does your vision have anything to do with the missing girls?" His question only brought a sense of emptiness. No knowledge or feelings came with it.

"No idea. The question might be too vague."

"Who's going to hurt Carly?" This question brought an answer, one I didn't like and had no intention of declaring. I shook my head, refusing to look at him, as I denied knowing the answer.

He persisted, almost as if he knew I knew something and wasn't telling him. "Who's going to physically hurt Carly?" The answer came at me again, insistent, and I ignored it, refusing to believe it. There was a chance, a slim one, that what I'd seen wouldn't come to pass, but either way, I didn't believe the man in front of me would be the one to hurt Carly.

He'd shown me his emotions, and I believed them more than the answer that persisted when he asked me who would hurt her. He was the one who would cause blood to stream down her face, and I refused to believe it, or tell him. He would never understand how easily moments in time could be misinterpreted, and I wouldn't give him something to feel guilty about, when it hadn't actually come to pass.

"It's late." I stood up, and he followed suit more slowly. I could tell he wanted to push, knowing I was hiding something, but he finally gave in.

He paused at the door, looking at me sympathetically. "Your gift … it's not really a gift at all, is it?"

I shook my head, telling him, "No, it isn't," and closed the door.

Chapter Nine

The next week followed much like the week before. I was accompanied by babysitters between every class. The only exception was Jules, who I hadn't seen in three days. I had the feeling she was dodging me, now that she knew I knew her secret.

Connor was his usual laidback self, leading me to suspect she hadn't brought it up to him. I wondered what she was waiting for, but since she wasn't around, I didn't have a chance to ask.

Jake seemed more and more tense, as the friction between him and his captain had grown, since they'd made the connection between the missing girls and the drowned kidnapper. Jake and Connor had managed to find the guy's car, and the evidence in it tied the missing girls to the drowning victim. The captain was suspicious as to why they'd bothered to look for a link, and refused to give the missing girls' cases to Jake and Connor, frustrating them further.

Danny was usually the one to escort us to our late class on Tuesday and Thursday, since he had to come after work to do his bodyguard duty. On Tuesday, he'd surprised me by asking Carly out to dinner, after bringing us to my dorm. He usually walked Carly to her car and then walked me to the dorm, but this time he switched it up, and there was no doubt about what her response would be.

She'd called me the next morning on the way to class, gushing about their date. I had to hang up on her when class started, and she switched to texting me. We didn't share any classes on Wednesday, so she was limited to texting and waiting on my response, until I got out of class, a fact that seemed to aggravate her, based on the fifteen texts I had waiting for me when I finally did get out of class. I attempted to respond to them, while Connor escorted me to class, his hand around my elbow, leading me, since I wasn't paying attention to where we were going.

It wasn't until we arrived at my next class that I realized how unusual it was. Connor would normally be joking and telling me stupid shit to text to Carly. No way would he have been silent the entire way.

"Hey," I said, grabbing his arm as he turned to go, leaving me at the door without a word. His distraction was apparent when I gazed at him. He leaned over and kissed my forehead.

"I'll be back after class," he told me, his thoughts obviously miles away. I held on tighter to his arm, and he glanced at me, saying, "It's okay. We'll talk when I get back." I nodded slowly, concern catching me off guard. It wasn't often I had to worry about easy-going Connor, and I didn't like the feeling at all.

I walked into class, distracted by Connor's odd behavior, and it took me a few minutes to notice I was the only one in there. I finally noticed the note on the board, canceling class. It was odd wandering back outside, and not having a bodyguard waiting for me. I knew I could call Connor and he'd come back, and I even debated calling Jules and using her overprotective nature to force her to stop avoiding me. In the end, though, I used my unexpected freedom to find some answers.

The bell jingled as I pushed the door open to the shop. Wade peeked around the curtain, surprise crossing his face as he saw it was me.

"You came back."

"I feel, as a self-proclaimed psychic, you shouldn't be so surprised by this."

He chuckled and gestured me toward the back room.

"You're an unusual one. I have a feeling I'll never be able to predict what you'll do." I stepped though the beaded curtain into the back room, seeing what I'd missed, when we'd left so abruptly. There was a cozy table in the corner with chairs, a counter with a coffee pot, and a couch. I must have interrupted him, because I could see the indention where he'd been sitting on the couch, a sketch book on the low table in front of his spot. "Grannie has been looking forward to your return. *She* had no doubts you'd be back."

"She seems like a smart woman," I murmured in reply, my attention once again drawn to the sketches on the wall. Dozens of questions tumbled through my head, questions I knew there'd be no answer to, if I asked them.

"You seem fascinated by my drawings."

I heard the question in the statement and replied, "Wondering if there are any unsolved mysteries here."

"Grannie believes you would be the one to ask." His words drew my attention to him, and I opened my mouth to ask him where she was, when I heard her light steps.

She didn't look surprised to see me, leading me to believe she'd known I was here. "Are you ready to learn?" I nodded, and she moved to the table, gesturing for me to sit next to her. With the three of us, the table was a tad crowded, but it wasn't uncomfortable. I felt at ease with both of them, a sense of familiarity between us.

"What is a truth seeker?" I asked her, the question eating at me over the last few days. It was a term I'd seen in her mind when she asked who I was, but there was no certainty behind it.

"One who can always ferret out the truth. No one can lie to a truth seeker. They always know. You saw that when I asked you who you were?" I nodded, and she sighed, relaxing back into the chair. "Then I imagine that's what you are. Truthfully, I never expected to meet another one."

Startled shock was written on my face as I said, "You've met someone with my ability?"

She smiled, memories overtaking her as she told me, "Once. I wasn't joking when I said you were a rare one indeed. I was barely six years old when my own grannie told me to come here and meet her friend. She told me, "I want you to meet this woman. She's a truth seeker, and it's not often you meet one with a gift such as this." She paused, looking me straight in the eye then. "That woman was older than my grannie, and she was the only truth seeker my grannie had ever met, and let me tell you, hers was a strong gift. It's been more years than I'll admit to you since then, but I haven't met another."

"What can you do?" I was curious about their abilities, which obviously differed from mine in some way.

"Mostly flashes of people's lives when I touch them, impressions you could say. Sometimes, I can sense when something is coming. The future is much more difficult to predict." I nodded, familiar with that. I glanced at Wade, wondering if his were the same or different.

"The same, except I can see auras, I guess you'd call them. A person's emotional state." He flicked his hand to the drawing of the cabin. "When you look at that, you feel a deep sadness, but it's twisted up with a strong sense of satisfaction." I realized his gift was subtle, but powerful.

Glancing around the room, listening to them speak of their extrasensory abilities, I felt a sense of belonging. It was the first time I'd been around people who had abilities similar to mine, or at least, people who immediately accepted my own gift with no question.

The ringing of my cell phone broke the silence, and I muttered, "Oh, crap" when I saw it was Connor.

"Hello."

"Where are you?" He was breathing heavily, like he'd been running, and it sounded like he was pacing. "I came back to your class and found out class was cancelled. So … Where. Are. You?" I sighed, unwilling to tell him about my new found psychic friends.

"I went to the store. I'm on my way back. I thought I'd get back before you showed up."

"Hurry up. Oh, and I don't I believe you, but we'll discuss that when you get here."

I stabbed the End button, muttering, "Over-protective asses."

I felt their curious stares, and I gave a sheepish smile. "I slipped my bodyguard to come visit. But he caught me." I waved the phone, still in my hand. "With the missing girls, my boyfriend and friends have been a little overprotective. Not surprising, since they're cops." They nodded, looking bemused, and I stood up. I wanted to come back here, to this place that seemed to understand what made me different. The sketches on the wall beckoned me; one in particular drew my attention. It felt a little awkward to ask, but I sucked it up and did it.

"Can I come back?"

"Of course, Addie." She smiled as I gave her a surprised look. "Names are the easiest thing to sense about someone. They are the call by which your essence answers, too."

I nodded, her explanation of a name one of the truest things I'd heard. I headed for the door, but a sketch on the wall stopped me. I stared at it, not understanding why it drew me. The sketch was nothing more than a wall with a door in it. It reminded me of ….

I spun around, and directed my comment to Grannie, "There's a door in my mind, and sometimes a question will rip it open.

There's darkness on the other side, so dense it feels like I could touch it, but it frightens me." I left out the part about the flashes I thought I'd seen inside of it. The flashing images that seemed to go forever and drew me to the door, curious as to what I'd find if I looked a little closer.

Grannie drew in a sharp breath, a warning on her face.

"That is a dangerous place, Addie. You must be very careful with a door like that. Never attempt to open it without someone who can pull you back. There are those who've been sucked into the darkness, believing answers lie there. Those people never found their way back out. Only by living can one find the truth."

I nodded, her warning coming loud and clear. She told me what I'd already begun to suspect. That door hinted at truths I never could have imagined, but the cost could be far too high.

The chirp of my phone startled me, and I saw a text from Connor, his impatience growing as he waited for me.

"Come back and we'll talk about it some more, but please be very careful if you see that door opening again. Don't seek it out, not without more knowledge." She was worried, and I sought to reassure her, "I won't. I promise."

My hand was on the door to leave, when I felt a gentle touch on my arm. Wade gazed at me uncomfortably.

"I'm not sure I should say anything, but at the same time, if something does happen ..." I waited, figuring he'd seen something, perhaps a hint of the future, or something to do with the missing girls. "Your friend, the curly haired one; I have a bad feeling. Something is going to happen to her. I know it's ridiculously vague, but you have your own gifts, and maybe it makes more sense to you."

I nodded, shaken by his words. It seemed there was no escaping Carly getting hurt, but could I live with myself knowing it would be Danny who'd hurt her and I'd said nothing?

When I got back to the school, Connor was pacing the parking lot, and as soon as he saw my car, he came over. I was about to get out when he shook his head, pulling the car door open.

"No. We're going to the precinct. Another girl has been kidnapped." Connor rested his head back on the seat, and I put the car in gear, my heart thumping like crazy. I could barely push the words out, "Is it Carly?"

He turned suddenly and scrutinized me. "No, a girl named Madison. Why would you think it was Carly?" His question caused me to lose focus for a second, the memory of why I thought it was Carly flashing through my mind.

"Stop!" he shouted, and I hit the brake, barely missing the car in front of me. "Okay, put it in park. I'll drive. And you'll tell me why you think it was Carly and where you've been. Secrets don't make friends, Addie."

As he drove us to the precinct, I told him about the dream and the other psychics I'd met.

"Holy shit, woman. Does Jake know?" I shook my head, and he frowned at me. "You know better than that. Secrets are like a poison, Addie. They wind up hurting everyone." He looked tired and serious, two looks I rarely saw on Connor.

"Jules told you?" I guessed, and he gave me a quick sideways glance as he nodded.

"I found out by accident," I admitted, holding up my hands in my own defense. "Granted, that's how I find out a lot of things."

"Yeah, you knowing doesn't bother me." One hand clenched the steering wheel, while the other drummed an incessant beat.

"But something is bothering you," I prodded, knowing he needed to say whatever was on his mind.

"Why would she wait to tell me something so huge? It hurts her, but she's never told me. Why? Can you tell me why, Addie?" He burst out, his quick glance accusing before going back to the road. I was grateful he'd taken over the driving, with the questions he was throwing at me. His pain thrummed through me, keeping cadence with the drum of his fingers. It tasted of betrayal, her decision not to tell him she couldn't have children, not because he cared about having kids, but because she didn't trust him with it.

"Connor, she didn't tell you, because she knew it wouldn't change anything." I laughed when I saw the confused look on his face. He glared at me, a frown forming at my levity. "I'm ... trying to explain, but it's kind of amusing." His frown only grew, so I hurried. "You come in like a wrecking ball, Con."

"Miley Cyrus? That is where you went with this?" He fought the smile that was attempting to form. "I'm trying to be serious for once here. I don't care that she can't have babies, but she does care. And I feel like I've been left out of this huge secret. And I want to know why."

"Sometimes, Connor, we hide the things that hurt us. We hide them so deep we can't feel them and taking them out to talk about them ... well, it hurts." Tears formed in my eyes. We all had those things we didn't want to deal with. My grandmother's death was mine. Jules' pain was like that. She'd known for a long time she couldn't have babies, but talking about it was like poking a sore tooth. It caused nothing but pain.

"Oh, don't cry! I'm serious now. Do *not* cry." Connor threw me a panicked look, and I started to laugh, sniffing back the tears.

"Connor, she loves you completely. Not telling you ... it had nothing to do with you. And I know how that sounds. But she

105

loves you so much, it doesn't matter that she can't get pregnant. You are worth it. Any other guy and she would have brought it up the second it was getting serious, but she didn't feel that way with you."

"What? She didn't think I would ever be serious?"

His hurt was coming through loud and clear, and I knew I was fucking this up ten ways to Sunday.

"NO!" I pounded my hand on the armrest, and he glanced at me in surprise. "It was a non-issue with you. GRRRR. I'm not explaining this right." I sighed, took a deep breath, and prayed for the right words. "This is Jules, Ms. Planner Extraordinaire, and to you, the word *plan* is practically an insult. You smashed her perfect little world into pieces." He looked at me, and I hurried to clarify. "In the best way possible, of course." He still looked disbelieving, and not for the first time, I cursed this ability of mine. "You changed everything. She took the biggest risk of her life with you, and for her, it's always been serious, but she knew you weren't the type to leave. No matter what. Her not telling you was more about her own inability to deal with the fact, not because she didn't trust you with it." I reached over and stilled the fingers he continued to drum. "Natalie announcing she was pregnant forced her to confront her feelings, and trust me when I say they are complex and confusing and painful. But never for one second did she think you'd walk away because of it. We all know you're not that guy."

"I love her." His words were rough, emotion making them raw. "She's so strong. Damn near invincible even. I never even suspected there was this pain inside of her. Shouldn't I have known?"

My fingers tightened on his. "No, Con. You couldn't have. *I* had no idea. That's the thing with loving people, it takes a lifetime to discover everything about them."

He gripped my hand, threw me a quick sideways glance, and said, "What would I do without you?"

"Fall into a deep depression, move into the mountains to be a hermit, and eventually succumb to pneumonia, dying alone."

"I really have to stop asking questions I don't want the answers to," he muttered, letting go of my hand as I shrugged.

"So, why are we going to the precinct? You said another girl was kidnapped."

"Yes, and Jake wants you to listen in on the interview. Maybe you'll hear something we don't," Connor answered, not bothering to add they were desperate to resort to this. It was rare that I went to their office. Usually, if they were stumped, we'd go to the crime scene after it had been cleared, or they'd ask me questions, until something clicked.

"Who are you interviewing?"

"It's not us, actually. Nash is conducting the interview with the person who reported her missing. He's agreed to let us listen in." I cut my eyes toward him. "This is bad."

"Yes," he replied simply, turning into the police station.

He escorted me through the labyrinth of the precinct, stopping when he came to their desks. They were butted up to one another, similar to a dozen other desks arranged in the large room.

"Jake must be talking to Nash." Connor pointed to a seat. "I'll go see what's going on and be right back. Stay here."

I nodded, looking around the room curiously. I thought it'd be louder, busier maybe. There wasn't even a single person in handcuffs. My perusal was cut short when a voice said, "Can I help you?"

I examined the man in front of me. He was frowning, a perpetual look for him, I was sure. He wore a suit and tie, but it wasn't formal, more a casual nod to regulation. He was tall with a wiry build, and quite unexpected. His question had been impatient, and his expression was equally unpleasant, but the intent behind the question was kind. He truly wanted to know if I needed assistance, and would provide it if I did.

"I'm waiting on Jake," I answered, when it became obvious my mental musings had delayed me from answering in the normal time-frame. If anything, his frown became even heavier, and I wondered if anyone had ever told him his face was going to get stuck like that.

"Professional or personal?" he asked, to which I replied cheekily, "Both."

His eyebrows lowered, furrowing his brow and explaining the deep lines there. "Miss …" He paused, but I didn't fill in the blank with my name, so he continued. "You may find yourself amusing, but this is the wrong place to play around. Now, tell me why you're here."

"I'm Jake's girlfriend. I live on campus, and he wanted to talk to me about the missing girls." I skated by with tidbits of the truth, not wanting to give more information than necessary, but seeing no reason to lie. The man in front of me was eager to know more about Jake, and I was curious to know why. His words and expressions were contradictory to the feelings I got when he asked his questions.

"Captain." Jake and Connor walked up at that moment, answering more than a few questions for me. The dour man in front of me turned to greet them, and I saw him in a new light. This was the man making life difficult for Jake and Connor, but he was also curious about them.

"Kincaid, Hayes," he nodded to them, a frown fixed to his face, and I could start to see why Jake and Connor had their backs up around him. "Miss ..." I relented, knowing who he was now and suspecting the tension between all of them was nothing more than miscommunication.

"Michaels. Addie Michaels," I replied, sticking my hand out for him to shake. He appeared momentarily surprised, but took my proffered hand in a firm grip.

"It's nice to meet you, Addie Michaels." He turned to go, the tense men beside me not encouraging lingering.

"Captain." He paused, half turning at my calling of his title. "Someone has to take the first step." His gaze was sharp as he took a deep breath and responded.

"So, they do, Miss Michaels. So, they do." He gave a short nod and quickly walked across the room to a glass office, one that gave him a clear view of all the desks.

"Do I want to know?" Jake took my hand in his, squeezing it gently, and I shook my head slowly.

"Not right now."

"Never a dull moment with you, Miss Michaels," Connor teased, and I raised an eyebrow at him. It seemed to me, my life was extraordinarily dull, except for my choice of friends.

Two hours later, and we were no closer to finding anything. The interview had been a bust. The boyfriend that had reported the girl missing was useless. He didn't know anything and spent most of the time crying. It had been uncomfortable to watch, and the interviewing officer had finally left in disgust.

"We have three missing girls, and the kidnapper of the first two is dead."

"Who kidnapped the third one then?"

They both looked at me, but I shook my head. There was a man, but he had a hood on, his face cast in shadow, making it impossible for me to discern any features. Not even a name drifted through my mind. I blinked, clearing my next thought, almost before it could form. The man had seemed familiar to me. The set of his shoulders, his stance, something about him reminded me of someone.

"Addie?" His concern drew me from my thoughts, and I attempted a smile.

"I can't see him. Whoever it was. It was like his face was in shadow."

"Okay." Jake drew me toward him, giving me a quick, comforting hug, and stepped back. He wasn't one to be openly affectionate where he worked. His hug surprised me and made me wonder how upset I must have looked. This case seemed to get more muddled, and with no answers in sight, I feared for the girls who had been taken. I worried we were running out of time. They could disappear, and we would never find them.

"Why kidnap so many girls here? It doesn't make sense. It's a risk. We know there have been three kidnapped girls, and we're alert now." My frustration was evident to them, and Jake slid his hand up and down my arm, in an attempt to soothe me.

"We know," he answered patiently. "And now, with evidence tying the kidnapper's car to two missing girls, everyone else is starting to figure it out."

I nodded, feeling deflated. It was difficult for me to realize other people didn't see things like I did. They didn't hear the subtle lies their questions hinted at. They didn't get the constant barrage of extra information even a normal conversation resulted in for me. They didn't know what I knew, and sometimes, that was the most frustrating thing of all.

"We have a couple things to wrap up. If you wait, one of us will drive you home."

"I thought we were doing our defense training tonight?" We usually met once a week, but with everything going on lately, we'd missed a couple sessions. I'd told Carly to meet us tonight. I wanted to make sure we were prepared for whatever might come our way.

"Oh, yeah."

"You forgot."

"I did, but you just reminded me." Jake gave me a devastating smile in apology, the one that hinted at a dimple, and I caved. It was difficult, if not impossible to even pretend to be angry with him, when he gave me that smile.

"In that case, I'm going to head over to the gym. I have no doubt Jules will already be there beating up on some hapless guy who thought she was a lightweight," I told them, tired of being escorted everywhere.

"Are there any left at our gym?" Connor asked, looking doubtful.

"There's always a newbie," I replied, catching Jake's eye. He nodded, understanding my desire for independence, even if it was only to drive myself from one babysitter to another. He leaned close and whispered in my ear.

"I promise we'll stop these guys. Just a bit longer." I nodded, feeling the brush of his lips against my cheek. Connor started making kissing sounds behind us, and my breath puffed out.

"Also, you can beat the shit out of Connor tonight," he added, loudly enough that Connor heard.

"Wait, what?" Connor stammered. "No, no. You and Addie spar. Me and Jules. That's how it works."

111

"What, Con? You scared of little ol' me?" I smiled at him, reminded I owed him a couple hard hits for some of the more embarrassing moments he'd subjected me to lately.

"Of course not," he answered, his eyebrows drawn together. I laughed, and Jake grinned at how unconvincing he sounded.

"Walk me to my car?" He nodded, taking my hand and telling Connor he'd meet him back at their desk.

"Planning to have your wicked way with me before I have to go back to work?" he drawled with a smirk.

"Kinky, Officer Kincaid," I responded with a teasing look, my mind filled with images triggered by his question. "Quite a few fantasies you've had about me at work."

He chuckled, "Just a couple."

He let me swing our hands back and forth, even though I know it made him feel silly. It was something I did without thinking, finding it soothing, and it'd taken Jake a few months to get used to it. He mainly had, because I found it impossible to break the habit. He'd stop our arms from swinging, but a few minutes later, I'd start again. I think he finally just gave up and let me have it.

He tugged on my hand as I went to turn right.

"We're leaving," I said, pointing to the right where I thought the exit was.

"We are. It's this way." He jerked his head in the opposite direction as I muttered, "Dang it."

He laughed, letting go of my hand to wrap his arm around my shoulders.

"Now I know why you wanted me to walk you out. It wasn't to sneak in kisses, but so you wouldn't become forever lost in here and have to get a desk sergeant to help you out."

I peeked up at him from the crook of his shoulder.

"I'm going to have to break up with you now." He cocked an eyebrow at me. "You know me too well. You've discovered all my terrible flaws."

"And I love them all," he replied, pulling me down a side hall. He scanned both directions to make sure no one was around as he ducked his head and kissed me. This was no quick peck, but a full onslaught. I wound my fingers around his neck, cupping the back of his head as his mouth opened against mine. Our tongues explored as his hands ran down my back, settling for a moment on my hips and then sliding up again. My fingers played in the waves of hair at the nape of his neck, mussing his work look. I felt him pull away for a second, and then he was back, his lips running along my collarbone as his thumb raised the edge of my shirt to skim along the bare skin of my side.

"Jake," I murmured, tugging on his hair to pull his head up.

"Addie," he replied, his voice a low rumble that sent shivers through me. He obliged me by lifting his head, and I smiled, pressing a kiss against the underside of his chin, a spot I was well aware made him lose control.

"Minx," he growled, his mouth on mine in a second, his body pushing me against the wall, so all I felt was him pressed against me. The kiss was an attempt to devour me, and I let him, wanting to be devoured. My hands found their way to his sides, and I hugged him to me tighter, feeling every hard part of him against my softness. This had been one of his fantasies, and I was more than happy to fulfill it with him.

He lifted his lips from mine with a gasp, and both of us took the opportunity to breathe.

"You're a dangerous woman, Addie Michaels." I felt his lips skim my cheekbone up to my forehead.

"Me? I do believe you are the one who is mauling me in a police station hallway."

"And are you enjoying the mauling?"

"If you find that empty interview room you were fantasizing about earlier; I'd be more than happy to show you how much I'm enjoying it."

A low groan escaped him, and I watched him look up and down the hallway, considering it, before he finally shook his head.

"Like I said, dangerous." He winked, pressing a quick, hard kiss against my lips and drew me back into the main hallway.

Chapter Ten

"Ow!"

"Damn it! I told you I was sorry."

"Jesus, Jake. Call your woman off."

One more solid punch to the gut, and I stepped back, grinning.

"I'd say that would teach you not to embarrass me, but it won't. However, it was very satisfying." Our audience chuckled, and Connor finally felt safe enough to rip the padded helmet off and spit out the mouth guard.

"Jules! You didn't even attempt to protect your man." He held his hands up in a 'what the hell' way, and Jules shook her head.

"I love you, baby, but she was determined. And I know better than to piss her off." She smiled and tossed him a towel to wipe the sweat off.

We'd been sparring for the past two hours, taking turns practicing defensive and offensive moves with one another. Each of us had our own strengths and style, so working with everyone helped us develop multiple techniques. In a fight, you couldn't predict who your opponent was going to be, but practicing with multiple opponents made it easier to predict what an unknown might do.

"Can we call it a night?" Connor worked to get his gloves off, tangling the tape wrapped around his hand and getting stuck. Jules came to his rescue, teasing him, "You aren't tired, are you?"

"More like my ego can't handle any more today," he muttered, throwing me a cross look. I laughed and mouthed, "Mountain man." He shuddered, and heaved Jules to him in a hug.

"Oh, God. You stink, sir," she told him, laughing as she tried to wriggle away. It only served to encourage him though, as he rubbed on her, not releasing her, until she cried, "Uncle."

"Same time next week?" There were a couple groans, namely from Connor, but everyone nodded. Our regular practices kept us prepared, mentally and physically. So far, we'd been lucky and hadn't needed to use the training, but I had a feeling our luck was running out. I glanced over at Carly, who was smiling at something Danny had said to her. My gaze slid to him, and I wondered if I was doing the right thing. My instincts warred with my mind, where he was concerned.

A nudge drew me from my thoughts, and Jules gave me an enquiring look. I reached over, giving her a sideways hug, and she reciprocated.

"You're not mad?" I felt her worry in the question, and shook my head.

"Of course not. We're friends. Are you mad, because I found out without you telling me?" My look was droll, and she opened her mouth to respond before closing it, smiling.

"Good point. And no." She paused, and gave me a painful smile. "It's hard to talk about. You'd think by now it wouldn't be, but …."

"Now you have a reason to regret the fact," I said, knowing she wished she could have a child with Connor.

"He'd be such a great dad," Jules admitted, her words raspy with unshed tears.

"There are other possibilities," I attempted to encourage her. Jules was normally driven to succeed, but this felt insurmountable to her at the moment. Her head bobbed, and I wrapped my arms more tightly around her.

"You've got me, kid." This garnered a rough chuckle from her.

"Will we ever have a baby of our own?" The question spilled from her in a rush, and I know it had been weighing on her. As often as I told them I couldn't answer questions about the future, it was difficult to resist the urge, especially when the question was so personal.

"I don't know." It hurt to admit to her that I didn't know. I couldn't see anything from her question beyond her desperate desire to know. I wished I could lay to rest that last worry she had about marrying Connor, and tying him to her with no possibility of children.

"I just wish …"

"I know. I wish I could give you the answer."

The door in my mind beckoned, and I knew then it's true threat. To know, to give peace to Jules, made me consider opening the door. My friends around me could draw me back, but at what risk? I fought the urge to find out, resisting the allure of finding what the future held for us. The reasonable part of me knew how risky that path would be, and it fought with my emotions.

"Addie!" Connor called, tearing me from my dangerous thoughts.

"He bellows for you," Jules commented, a small moue forming. I laughed, untangling our arms and walking over to him.

I jumped on him, forcing him to catch me, as I clung like a monkey to his neck. He shifted me, so I was riding piggyback.

"I promise to go easy on you next week," I told him, tugging on his hair. He groaned, letting go of one of my legs to rub his ribs.

"You damn near broke me today," he said, hunching over and hamming it up.

"Good, you deserved it."

"Maybe."

"No maybe about it."

He twisted his head slightly, trying to catch a glimpse of my face, so I popped my head around.

"What happened with Jules? Y'all good?" I nodded, thinking about his questions.

"You gonna tell me?" I sighed, considering. It was going to tear him up knowing what she'd asked me, but at the same time, I thought he should know what he was up against.

"She asked if y'all would ever have a baby of your own."

I caught the pain on his face as he turned his head. I squeezed him extra tight around his shoulders where I was hanging on. "I couldn't see, but you know I can't see the future."

"It doesn't bother me!" he burst out, keeping his voice low, so we wouldn't be overheard. "The kid thing. We'll adopt, or we won't. I'd rather spend my life with Jules, instead of any other woman who might be able to give me kids."

"I know. I hear you loud and clear. But she thinks you'd make a great dad, and it's got her all twisted up."

"Well, she needs to be untwisted," he declared, to my amusement.

"I can't think of a better man for the job."

"You're right."

"Always, but what's going on in that head of yours?"

"The proposal."

I closed one eye, trying to figure out the leap in conversation.

"Ooookay?"

He huffed, twisting to look at me, and then unceremoniously dropped me. I landed on my feet, my cat-like reflexes saving me, plus the fact he'd crouched down and I'd dropped maybe two inches didn't hurt.

"The proposal has to be perfect. It has to show her that she's it for me. Babies or no babies, we're in this together—forever. She's what I dream about."

I sighed, still surprised when Connor managed to say the exact right thing.

"Remember that. Because I think you nailed the words. Any woman would be swept away by a proposal like that."

"It's just how I feel. I don't do pretty words very well."

"You don't need to," I told him with a shrug. "Sincerity trumps pretty words any day."

"But I want those too. It's gotta be the whole package. She deserves it. I want her to know she is all I ever want in this life."

Traitorous dampness filled my eyes, and I attempted to wipe it away before he saw. Stupid Connor and his heartfelt words.

"Are you crying?" He was incredulous, and I sniffed.

"No," I lied, straight to his face and redirected the conversation. "So, do you have an idea of how you want this proposal to go?"

"Not yet. Well, I have ideas. But I need you to find out what she really wants. And rings. You gotta help me find the perfect ring."

I gave a deep sigh, as if he was asking way too much, but the crestfallen expression on his face wouldn't let me keep up the act.

I saluted him, and his head jerked in surprise.

"I accept this mission, and will not falter in my task. I will work tirelessly to discover the information you seek." He shook his head, but smiled at my antics.

"See that you do," he replied sharply, and I nodded, turning on my heel to go back to Jake.

We watched everyone leave as we walked to my car. He'd ridden with Connor over to the gym, so I was taking him back to his apartment.

"Stay with me tonight?" he asked, playing with my hand in his.

"I have an early class tomorrow," I replied, toying with him. "Whatever will people think if I show up wearing the same clothes I had on today?"

"That you have a very lucky boyfriend?"

I laughed, knowing I would stay. It was surprising he still had any clothes left, because my borrowing tended to turn into never giving back. I wore his clothes more often than my own.

We stepped into the elevator, and after pressing the button for his floor, he spun me around. Our lips met, and I leaned against him, his legs spread, so I nestled between them.

"All afternoon, I've thought about you and me."

"In an elevator? Really? I'm learning all kinds of things about you today," I whispered, as his lips traced a trail down my neck, settling into the curve, and he kissed a spot that made me gasp. He chuckled, his lips moving against the sensitive skin.

"Elevator, bed, office, car. You name it and I'm there," he murmured against my ear, his hot breath sending a shiver through me, or maybe it was his words.

The ding of the elevator opening interrupted us, but luckily, we'd only arrived at his floor and hadn't embarrassed any old ladies. He picked me up, and I wrapped my legs around his waist. He kept kissing me as he walked us down the hall to his door. I drew his face toward mine, deepening the kiss, needing his tongue against mine. He pressed me against the door, his hand against my ass as he gave me what I demanded. I heard his keys hit the floor as his other hand brushed against my breast. I arched, and he flicked his thumb against my nipple.

"Jake," I moaned, my legs tightening around his hips, causing him to thrust against me lightly. He dragged his lips from mine, nipping my lower lip.

"I need to get us inside before I have to explain to the new captain why I was arrested for indecent exposure."

He shifted, leaning down to get the keys he'd dropped, placing his head level with my breasts. He brushed his lips across them, and my nipples puckered at the light sensation. A second later, he had the key in the door and we were inside.

A few steps later, and I was pressed into the couch, his heavy weight on top of me. I slid one of my legs down his, tangling us together as our lips met and our tongues dueled. My hands found themselves under his shirt, running along the planes of his back, the heavy muscles shifting as he kept his weight from crushing me.

I pushed the shirt up, wanting him to take it off, and he shifted up, grabbing the neck of it with one hand and pulling it off in a quick motion. He reached down, sliding both of his hands under my shirt and working it up. He made sure to touch every inch of me as he pushed it up, sliding his hand around my back to unhook my bra, while he was at it.

He leaned down, pressing his mouth to my bare stomach, when we heard the phone ring. I felt his groan against my skin as he sat up.

"You've got to fucking be kidding me." My laugh was only slightly frustrated. We'd been interrupted more than once by his work. "Where is my phone?" He scanned the room, still kneeling between my legs and shirtless, so I enjoyed the view of his muscles as he twisted around, finally spotting his phone on the side table where he'd dumped his keys.

"Kincaid," he barked, more than a little frustrated by our interruption, based on the large bulge I could see pressing against the soft cloth of his workout pants. His finger traced a pattern on my stomach as he listened, and I could tell it was an address. Jake swore that writing or tracing the numbers helped him to remember them. "Alright, I'll be there in a few." His expression was contrite as he gazed down at me, closing his eyes momentarily as the bulge in his pants twitched. A smile flickered across my lips, knowing he had no desire to leave. He leaned down, giving me a hard kiss and a promise to be back soon. Moments later, he'd tugged on his shirt and was out the door.

I straightened my clothes and hopped up to take a shower. Might as well get the sweat from our earlier workout off, since we weren't working up to another one. He wasn't back by the time I finished showering, so I knew he'd be late getting in. I sprawled back on the couch, wearing one of his t-shirts and flipped the television on.

Hours later, I was awakened, when he picked me up.

"Shh, go back to sleep," he whispered, placing a gentle kiss on my forehead. I rested my head on his shoulder as he cradled me in his arms, asleep again before he'd even laid me on the bed.

Chapter Eleven

"Penny for your thoughts."

His soft words caught me by surprise. It was still dark outside, and I thought he was asleep. Perhaps tracing my fingers over his chest had woken him up.

Oops.

I snuggled my head against him, and he placed a kiss against my hair.

"I'm not sure. A penny for all of my thoughts? Seems a little cheap to me. Maybe a penny per thought," I replied, trying to sort out the tangle of thoughts that were keeping me awake when I should be sleeping. I felt him reach over to the nightstand and a few seconds later say,

"Eighty-seven."

I tilted my head up inquiringly, and he held out his hand. I cupped my own hand, and he poured the change into it.

"Eighty-seven cents. So, I believe that affords me eighty-seven thoughts." I curled my fingers to keep the money from escaping, and smiled.

"Connor wants help proposing to Jules." I felt him start in surprise, and remembered he didn't know about the whole marriage thing.

Well, damn.

"I met a couple psychics. Real ones." This time, I felt his head turn, but kept going. "I had a vision. Of the future. One I think is real."

"And?" he asked, knowing this was the one weighing on me the heaviest.

"It was Carly. She was hurt, and I don't know when or why." He held me tighter, as tears escaped me. He ran his finger over my cheek, catching them.

"Anything else?"

"I think Danny is the one that's going to hurt her." The next words spilled out in a rush, unable to be contained any longer. "And there's a door in my head, one that could give me the answers, but the cost ... I don't know what the cost would be." I bit my lip as I admitted the last piece, ashamed that my fear outweighed my desire to protect Carly.

"The cost is too high. It's dangerous, that's what you're telling me." I nodded my head against his chest, unwilling to look at him. "Addie, knowing what *might* happen is not worth you endangering yourself. Any of us would tell you that. Including Carly."

"But what if she ... what if something happens to her, and I didn't do everything in my power to stop it?"

"Sweetheart, I love you, but you're putting too much pressure on yourself. This ability of yours—it's a gift. One that has helped us on multiple occasions, but visions are not exact, and not a one of us thinks differently. What you see might happen—*might*—and we both know the future can change. You've proven that." He tilted my chin up, forcing me to meet his eyes. "This door you're talking about; it's opened before, hasn't it?"

I nodded, unable to break the stare he had me locked in. "Jules was the first to open it. That night." I waved my hand and sat cross-legged next to him. "She asked the question, and it was suddenly there. Nothing but a black void." He rested his hand on my thigh, his thumb stroking my skin. "The next time, I was at Mom's. She asked me something, and I woke up on the floor, with her screaming in my face." His face was tight with worry, or maybe fear, emotions I was becoming intimately familiar with myself. "That time, I saw flashes in the blackness. Images. I think they were the future and the past. Just infinite possibilities." His fingers had tightened on my leg with my words, and I set my hand on his. "The psychics ... they're a guy and his grandmother. She told me to leave the door alone. Never open it, unless someone could pull me back."

He was shaking his head, even as I said it. "No, that door stays shut. Do you hear me?" He leaned forward, his face in mine. "Possibilities. You said it yourself. Infinite possibilities. You could lose yourself in a place like that. And the risk isn't worth it. Not for a chance to know what *might* happen." He held my gaze, and the turmoil of his own emotions, the knot of fear, worry, and anxiety he felt at the thought of losing me to my own mind, slammed into me with his unintended question. I swayed at the force of them, my own face reflecting his emotions.

"I'm sorry." He cupped my face, kissing my cheek. "So sorry. I didn't mean to push my emotions onto you. I should have been more careful." I felt his head shake against my cheek. "The idea of a door in your mind, one that could be opened with a stray question. God, that's terrifying."

"I know." My hands gripped him, and he tugged me on to his lap. "But it's better now."

"How could it be better?" he asked, his confusion apparent.

"You know now. We can face it together." I ran my fingers over the rough stubble on his cheek. "You can pull me back, if the door opens. I know without a doubt; *you* can bring me back."

He blinked his eyes closed for a second. "Your faith amazes me." He hugged me close, and I ran my lips along his jaw, the prickle from his stubble tickling my skin. It was a relief to have everything out in the open. I hadn't realized how heavy the secrets had become, and while telling Connor had relieved some of the burden, it was nothing compared to Jake knowing. He'd been the first person I'd ever revealed my ability to, and in many ways, was the only one who understood the toll it took on me.

"And what do you mean, Connor wants help proposing?" I winced, hearing the betrayal mixed with anger in his voice, and sought to soothe him.

"He's going to ask your permission. He just wants a perfect proposal. He thinks Jules deserves it." I gave him a confident smile as he grumbled, "She damn well deserves it, putting up with him."

"This is true."

"Damn, he's going to be my brother-in-law." I laughed as he shook his head. "I don't know how I feel about that."

"She loves him, and he loves her. You should feel good about it," I told him, pressing a kiss against his lips. He kissed me back, his lips moving against mine intently as his hand slipped under the t-shirt I was wearing. He ran his hand along my hip, shifting me forward as I wound my hands around his neck. His other hand brushed the bottom of my breast, causing my nipples to tighten, and I moaned. The sound had him flipping me on my back, his mouth pressed against my neck as his hands roamed freely under the shirt.

The blare of the alarm interrupted us, and he stared at me in disbelief. "You've got to fucking be kidding me." He peered down at the bulge tenting his sleep pants and shook his head. "At this rate, I'm going to run out of baseball stats to recite." I laughed, my own frustration overridden by the exasperation on his face.

"You think this is funny? Do you?" I saw his intent, but it was too late, as he'd started tickling me, catching one of my flailing feet in his hand and making me laugh helplessly as he tickled me remorselessly.

"Stop, please. Uncle, uncle!" I cried, my stomach hurting from laughing and trying to twist away from him.

"Nope. Not the right answer," he said, continuing to torment me.

"Jake is the best boyfriend ever," I tried, breathless as I said it.

"Getting warmer."

"Best looking?"

"Not bad."

"Best lover!"

"Hmmm, that'll do." He stopped tickling me, grinning as I attempted to catch my breath. "See if you laugh the next time you miss out on a life-altering orgasm."

I grinned at his proclamation, knowing he could live up to his own hype. "I'm going to hold you to it, good looking." I gave him a wink, and darted into his closet to steal clothes. After I got dressed, I went into the bathroom to drag a brush through my tangled hair.

I whistled when I saw Jake, a towel wrapped around his waist as he shaved over the sink. Didn't matter that I'd seen him shirtless a few minutes earlier, there was something about a man wearing nothing but a towel that was as sexy as hell. He cut a sideways glance at me, never missing a stroke as the side of his mouth rose in a smirk.

Brushing only served to increase the wild waves in my hair, so I finally gave up, pulling the mass into a high ponytail and then swiped his chap stick across my lips. He rinsed his face, and tapped my hand before I could leave the bathroom. I gazed at him questioningly. It would be a miracle, if I wasn't late already. He smiled, pressed a kiss into my wrist and gestured to the granola bar and water he must have grabbed for me.

"Breakfast."

I smiled happily, and brushed a kiss against his smooth cheek. "Best boyfriend ever."

I wound up being late for class, but luck was on my side, since the professor was even later. When class let out, Jules and Carly were both waiting outside the door, to my surprise.

"To what do I owe this pleasure?" I joked, falling in between them. They traded a mischievous look, alerting me to the fact they were conspiring without me. It was an odd realization. They were starting to become friends outside of their friendship with me. I smothered the tiny flare of jealousy I felt, and looped my arms in theirs. "Obviously, y'all are up to something. I'm almost afraid to ask what."

"Someone's birthday is coming up," Carly told me.

"It's not mine," I replied with a grin. "It's also not Jake's or Jules or yours. So that leaves Danny and Connor. Wait. Why do I not know when Connor's birthday is?"

"Cause, he absolutely hates to celebrate it, and refuses to tell anyone when it is. But ..."

"We figured you would know."

"But I don't."

They gave me pitying looks, and it dawned on me.

"It's early. What can I say ... I didn't get much sleep last night."

"Oooohhh, spill." Carly grinned, and Jules held up a hand. "Wait a minute, this is my brother. I don't want to know."

I laughed at them. "Trust me, I wish. Jake had to go out on a call late, and then I couldn't sleep this morning."

"Oh. That's disappointing," Carly muttered. "How can I live vicariously through you, if you don't do anything worth hearing about?"

"I don't know. You and Danny boy seemed pretty tight last night," Jules chimed in, arching an eyebrow.

Carly flushed and ducked behind her unruly mass of hair. I took pity on her and distracted Jules with my earlier question I hadn't got to ask.

"Why does Connor hate celebrating his birthday?"

"We don't know."

"Hmm, a mystery."

"Not for long."

They giggled, and I hoped whatever reason Connor had for not celebrating his birthday wasn't too terrible, because I didn't want to have to be the one to ruin their fun.

"Come on, let's get breakfast."

"I had a granola bar already."

"Ha, that's not a sufficient breakfast."

"Nope. But you know what is?"

I sighed, seeing the answer and admitting defeat.

"Cinnamon rolls!"

"To the Bakery, we go."

A few minutes later, we were squished together in a booth, with giant cinnamon rolls, smothered in icing, sitting in front of us.

"That sticky bun looked good."

"Bite your tongue. We are not sticky bun girls."

"We could branch out, try new things."

They both gave me horrified looks, so I threw my hands up. "Or not. We'll just eat cinnamon rolls." They both nodded, satisfied, and I muttered under my breath, "Jake would let me eat a sticky bun."

"What did you say?" Jules glared at me suspiciously, and I leaned back.

"Nothing."

"When is Connor's birthday?" Carly said around a mouthful of pastry. "This is really good, by the way."

"February twenty-eighth."

"That's Tuesday! We almost missed it."

"Wait. Tuesday? Like Fat Tuesday?"

"Uh, yeah."

"Oh my God, this will be awesome. We can do a whole Mardi Gras themed birthday party. Beads, King Cake. Jules, you can even lift your shirt up for a coconut." Carly started rattling off options excitedly.

"Carly! I'm not flashing anybody for anything."

"Poor Connor." My comment didn't go over well, as Jules swatted me.

"Poor Connor, my ass," she muttered, causing me to laugh as I started unraveling my cinnamon roll.

"Why must you do that?" Jules asked, watching me deconstruct the roll to eat it. I shrugged, not having an answer.

"She's always eaten them that way," Carly told her, cutting up her roll.

"Jeez, do none of you know how to eat a cinnamon roll?"

"I'm going to go with *that's a rhetorical question*." We watched Jules pick up her roll and take a bite. It was impressive, considering the roll was the size of her head.

"Okay, that was harder than I thought," she admitted, setting it back down, while trying to swallow the bite she'd taken.

"Solid nine."

"Absolutely. It was impressive, just seeing it. Connor doesn't know what he has in you."

She shook her head at us, but couldn't stop her smile.

"Okay, so we know when his birthday is, and we have a great theme, because it's how perfect? Right?"

Jules nodded, but stopped as I shook my head. Carly's question had revealed why Connor didn't celebrate his birthday.

"Connor will be pissed, if we celebrate his birthday with a King Cake," I told them with a sympathetic smile.

"Why does Connor hate celebrating his birthday?" Jules asked, with a resigned look.

"Because it's always King Cakes and Mardi Gras every year, even when his birthday doesn't fall on Mardi Gras. By the way, he despises King Cake, so I'd avoid that at all costs."

"But …. Dang it," Carly frowned, stabbing a bite of her cinnamon roll and shoving it in her mouth. I tore off another piece as I let them stew over this new knowledge.

"Maybe we should go classic. Something simple," I offered, when the silence had dragged on for an uncomfortably long time.

"Yes."

"Great."

They jumped on the suggestion as soon as I said it, discussing balloons, chocolate or white cake, and if he'd play pin the tail on the donkey.

"Yes, chocolate, and hell no. Are you kidding me?" I answered proudly. They both gave me exasperated looks and sighed. "What? Oh, you weren't asking me were you? Well, he's not gonna play pin the tail on the donkey. Maybe, pin the nipple piercing on the model."

We all laughed, and Jules stood up, gasping with laugher.

"I have to pee. You have laughed the pee right out of me."

This pushed us further over the edge, and I wiped tears from my eyes as Carly snorted. This set me off again, but I tried to control myself, needing to ask Carly a favor before Jules came back.

"Carly. Carly!"

"What?" She popped the last of her cinnamon roll in her mouth, and gazed at me with an expectant look.

"I need you to ask Jules what the perfect proposal is." This caused her to choke, and I pounded her on the back as she reached for her coffee.

"Well, okay. Connor's proposing?" She peered at me with wide eyes. "It is Connor, right? Like, it's not Jake. But no, why would you want to know what Jules' perfect proposal would be? It'd be yours, so it must be Connor." She gasped. "Unless there's someone else? Is Jules cheating on Connor?"

I stared at her with my mouth open.

"Where? Just where does this shit come from? Nobody is cheating. Jake is NOT proposing and yes, it's Connor."

"Oh, well why do I need to ask? Why don't you ask her?"

"Cause, she'll absolutely suspect me if I ask. I need you to ask when I get up to go the bathroom. I'll go around the corner and eavesdrop."

"Your ability will work like that?" she asked curiously, and I saw the answer.

"Yes. So long as I can hear the question, I'll see the answer."

"What would Jules perfect proposal be?" Carly asked, with an inquiring look. I shook my head, not seeing anything.

"I don't think it works like that."

"Worth a shot," Carly replied with a shrug. I nodded, always curious about the limits of my ability. Jules walked back over, and I hopped up.

"My turn."

I stepped around the corner and waited. It took a few minutes, but Carly finally got the conversation around to weddings and proposals.

"I think I'd want to be proposed to under the stars," Carly said dreamily, the man proposing looking quite a bit like Danny, if I wasn't mistaken. "What about you, Jules? What's the perfect proposal for you?" Jules glanced down, and Carly's eyes widened as I popped my head around the corner and nodded. I had what I needed. Connor, however, had his work cut out for him.

"Family. I want my family to be there," Jules said as I walked back to them and slid in next to her.

"For what?" I asked, innocently.

"My proposal," she answered, with a speculative look toward me. I gave her a guileless look, raising an eyebrow.

"Is someone proposing?"

"I don't know. Are they?" Her eyes narrowed.

"Touché."

"You're not going to tell me are you?"

"Nope."

We looked away from one another, breaking the stare-down we were locked in, only to meet Carly's amused stare.

"That was entertaining."

"And I'm going to be late for class," I replied, jumping up and collecting my bag.

"Wait. I have to walk you," Jules said, sliding out and hurrying to catch up.

"Then walk fast."

Chapter Twelve

My phone buzzed with an incoming text message from a number I didn't recognize. When I opened it, I knew immediately it was from Wade. It was a picture of a sketch he'd drawn quickly, the bold strokes almost appearing as if they had torn the page as he drew.

"I keep seeing this place. It has something to do with you."

"I don't recognize it," I typed back and then looked at the picture again. I expanded it, seeing what appeared to be a rundown shack, perched on stilts. Part of the shack was over the water, but I couldn't tell if it was a bayou or the river. Something told me this was where they were keeping the girls, but there were thousands of places exactly like this one. It would be like trying to find a needle in a haystack … unless you were able to answer any question.

"Do you know where it is?" he persisted, and I replied, "My ability doesn't work over text message. No idea why. I'll show my boyfriend. See if we can determine where this is."

"Okay, be careful."

I heeded his warning, glancing around my classroom, feeling unsettled, even as I stared at what might very possibly be the break we were looking for. I didn't hear a word of the lecture, as I watched the clock, my foot tapping impatiently. I considered leaving in the middle of class, but decided it wouldn't help matters. Connor or Jake would be outside the door waiting to escort me to lunch, once class ended. They would be able to ask me the all-important question, and hopefully it would lead us to the girls.

The second the clock hit the hour, I was out of my desk and jogging down the steps to the door. As soon as I stepped into the hall, I saw them. They were joking about something, standing by the window, completely oblivious to the college girls giving them flirtatious looks. The sun coming through the window gave Connor the appearance of having a halo, a misconception if ever I'd seen one. Jake caught sight of me first, a slow grin crossing his face as his eyes met mine. Relief trickled through me at seeing both of them. Maybe we could finally end the nightmare for those girls.

"Addie," Connor called, spotting me. "You tell us who's cooler. The Arrow or Flash?"

"Arrow," I responded automatically, knowing Connor preferred the Flash. I thrust my phone in Jake's face, causing him to shift back as he took it.

"Where is this?" He squinted at the picture, enlarging it. "What is this?"

"It's a shack on the river, off Highway 9. Twenty miles from here as the crow flies," I replied, knowing exactly where it was. It didn't matter that I'd never been there, I could find it with my eyes closed.

"What's there?" Connor asked, peering over Jake's shoulder at the picture. Tears of relief filled my eyes as I saw them.

"The girls. They're there." I pointed at my phone, at the sketch Wade had drawn, knowing something was there and trusting I would be able to figure it out.

"Are you sure?" Jake gazed at me intently, his face serious, and I nodded, completely positive all three girls were still there.

"We need to get a team out there."

"Is anyone guarding the girls?"

"Yes." Two men in shadow paced outside the door. Jake took my elbow, guiding me as we stepped outside into the cold. They were headed back to the precinct, so they could pull together a team capable of extracting the girls.

"How many?"

"Four. No, six." I focused, but the vision kept switching on me. It was difficult to tell if I was seeing the same people or different ones. Only two guarded the girls, but there were others.

"How many bad guys are there?" he clarified, understanding my struggle.

"Seven." My answer was confident now. I didn't know where they all were, but we could determine that with other questions.

"How many kidnapped girls are there?" Connor broke in.

"Five," I replied.

"Five?" Their disbelief was layered with anger, as they realized there were more out there than we'd known about, perhaps taken from other towns and held here, until it was time to ship them.

"We don't have time to waste. This is still technically Nash's case, but we need to move on it."

"How are we going to get the new captain to agree to authorize a hostage removal team? We know Addie, but what are we going to tell him? A tip? He's gonna give us hell."

Connor's questions blurred together as I saw the answer.

"Leave him to me," I managed to respond, grateful for Jake's support as we walked.

"Addie ..." I heard the warning, but shook my head.

"Trust me."

I met his eyes, and he nodded, saying, "I do."

"Okay then, let's go rescue some girls."

Jake turned on the lights and siren as we raced to the precinct. Connor made calls, letting them know to get a team ready. It took special equipment and training to move in on a known hostage situation, and these weren't your typical hostages. They were guarded to keep them from escaping, but could easily be killed, if the traffickers suspected they'd been made.

They'd move on to another town, kidnapping more girls to send to other cities, or even overseas, and we'd never capture them. We couldn't allow that to happen. I'd felt the same terror those girls felt, and I wouldn't rest, until someone paid for their pain.

"What do you think you're doing?" His face was just as unpleasant now as it was the first time I'd seen him, but again the question was genuinely curious. I was beginning to think the captain had resting bitch face, and it was definitely alienating his men.

"We are coordinating a team. We have information telling us where the kidnapped girls are located. It's well guarded, and we'll need to be cautious moving in."

"Where did you get this information? Shouldn't Nash be coordinating?" A lightbulb went off with the captain's question. It explained his constant reassigning of cases, a fact Jake and Connor had found insulting, on more than one occasion, as several of their cases had been taken from them.

"A reliable source, and I don't know where Nash is, but we need to go. We don't know when the girls will be moved." Jake worked to control his aggravation, but it was apparent in the muscle twitching along his jaw. He hadn't formed any type of relationship with the new captain, his feelings of betrayal spilling over from the previous captain, and the new captain wasn't much for relationship-building either.

"Who is the reliable source? If a move is being made on Nash's case, he needs to be involved." He was suspicious of the source, not wanting the department to look foolish, if the source—i.e. me—was wrong. The previous captain had shaken the community's faith in the police department, and the new captain wanted to improve people's perception.

"What difference does it make? Trust me to know the source is good, and we can't afford to wait on Nash. Are you going to authorize or not?" Jake was breathing heavily, his normally calm demeanor gone as Connor and half the department watched us, their eyes shifting from one to another. The showdown had finally happened, and it couldn't be at a worse time. I could see the captain's answer, and I knew there would be no coming back if he spoke the words aloud.

"Captain, it's good to see you again." I wedged myself in between the two, ignoring the wide eyed stares I was getting. Almost everyone knew who I was. I'd been the high school girl shot trying to protect two police officers, and that was if they didn't know me as Jake's younger girlfriend.

"Miss Michaels, you've returned, and right in the midst of a break in the case for the missing girls. Odd." He squinted at Jake challengingly. "Do you always bring your girlfriend along when you're trying to rescue hostages?"

There was no missing the bite in his question, and I winced in sympathy. He was calling Jake out for challenging him in front of his department. I could feel the tension rolling off of Jake, and knew this little argument needed to be stopped now.

"Gentlemen, there are *five* women being held captive twenty miles away from here. At any moment, they could be stuffed into a shipping unit and be out of our reach, never to be heard from again. While your pissing contest is entertaining, it's not solving the problem." I felt Jake jolt behind me, and his hand came around to cup my elbow. The captain was shocked by my outburst, and I leaned toward him, not breaking eye contact. "I am the source, and trust me when I say, they're where I say they are. Send the team. If by chance I'm wrong, at least you tried, based on a tip you received. If I'm right, and you will learn, I'm *always* right, then you just saved the lives of five terrified women." I paused, making absolutely sure he understood me. "If you don't go, I will, and they may not all make it, without the resources you have."

"You will give me a full explanation," he murmured, before raising his voice. "You have my authorization. I hope you are correct and these women's lives are saved by your efforts. I will be expecting a full report upon your return."

I felt Jake nod behind me, and then everyone was moving. Gear was loaded, and Jake and Connor were shrugging on Kevlar vests and hustling out the door. I raced to catch up, grabbing Jake's sleeve as Connor watched us.

"Babe, it's not safe. I don't want you anywhere near these guys. We don't know what we're walking into." I could see the resolve in his eyes as he continued. "These women … they could be hurt, badly. I don't want you to get caught up in their emotions."

"Jake!" I was exasperated, not by his concern, but by the more logical issue. "You can't find them without me."

His eyes closed in realization, and Connor guffawed next to us.

"She has us there, dude." Connor threw me the extra small Kevlar vest he was holding and winked. "Load up, buttercup. You're coming with us."

The drive was tense, with everyone aware the situation was potentially dangerous. The only sound was my occasional directions. It took us thirty minutes to get there, and we had to stop a distance from the turnoff, not wanting to tip off the guards patrolling by the road.

"Stay here." He gave me a pleading look. "Please."

I nodded, having no desire to be in the midst of them extracting the women. My presence would only distract Jake and Connor, endangering them further, and I had no desire to get shot again.

"Be safe," I urged him, fear for his safety always a concern.

"I will." My lips pressed against his, sealing his promise.

"Move out." The words came over the radio in the van where I was placed to wait, jolting us apart. He gave me a long look as he jumped out.

The wait seemed interminable, the radio stuttering to life periodically as the men moved into position, the staccato of gunfire interspersed with shouting, causing my heart to pound. My fists clenched so tightly, my knuckles turned white.

"Clear, clear."

"Perimeter is clear."

"Report in."

"We have them."

"Repeat."

"We have the girls secured."

"They are alive."

Relief rushed through me, tears spilling over, as I knew they were safe. I wrapped my arms around my knees, rocking back and forth as the tears soaked into my jeans. The van door jerked open, startling me, and Jake was there, dragging me into a hard hug.

"You were right. You saved them," he murmured, over and over, stroking my hair. "You did it."

"We did it."

Chapter Thirteen

"The girls will be okay. Thanks to you."

Wade shook his head at my words, a self-deprecating smile on his face.

"I drew a picture. I had no way of knowing where it was or what it meant. So it seems to me that you are the one owed the appreciation."

"I don't know. I'm not the one who went charging in with guns blazing and got them out. So truly, we should be thanking the officers." We both looked over at Jake and Connor sitting at the table with Grannie. She had insisted they get a reading when they walked in, stating their energy was so strong, it begged to be read.

"You have a point," Connor called, hearing us. "Trust the psychic. She's never wrong." I shook my head as Jake snorted. They wouldn't let me live it down, after telling the captain I was always right, and then we'd brought the girls in, making heroes out of the department. Hours of debriefings, and my own emotional exhaustion had granted me a temporary reprieve from giving the captain his explanation, but there was no question it was coming.

Jake insisted he'd support me in whatever decision I made. Connor had agreed, backing him up, and I knew they would. I could lie and tell the captain I'd overhead something on campus, but something in me resisted the idea. As I gazed around the tiny shop we were sitting in, owned by two people who unapologetically accepted who they were and what they could do, even knowing the ridicule they could be subjected to, made it difficult to continue denying who I was.

I'd been living in shadows for a long time, hiding an integral part of who I was from everyone I met, down to my own family. I didn't think I was ready to announce my ability to the world, but maybe it was time to start admitting it to the ones that mattered, to not hide what I could do. We'd saved lives using my skills, and seeing the sketches on the wall, I knew we could save more.

"Was he with you at the cabin?" Wade asked me in a low voice, not even bothering to point to the sketch he was referring to. He'd quickly grasped how my ability worked, accepting it easily as he asked me things.

"Yes, but you knew that." My look was curious, knowing there was more to the question, but Wade had the ability to cloak his questions, only asking the one he wanted an answer to. He thought my ability was growing stronger, which was why I could hear layers when a question was asked.

"I suspected," he corrected absently, watching Jake interact with his grandmother. "When he studied it, his emotions paralleled yours, with one exception."

I tilted my head, indicating he needed to expound on his comment.

"Protective. There was a strong element of protectiveness in his aura as he looked at it."

"Protectiveness is an emotion?"

"For some. Auras don't read as simply as a book. They have nuance and flow. Colors blend, as emotions cross over one another, flaring brighter as something is felt sharply."

"It sounds beautiful," I murmured, picturing a rainbow of emotion.

"Emotions aren't always easy to describe. Sometimes, they must be seen."

He gave me a thoughtful look and asked, "What does Jake's aura look like when he sees Addie?"

I could see then what he was referring to, and he was right. There was no way to describe the many hues a person's emotions could take. They swirled and blended into shades I'd never seen, and at the core, winding through Jake's aura, was a deep purple. It wasn't the typical color you'd associate with love, but I knew instinctively it represented his love for me. The color was created by blending red and blue, and as I studied it, I could see the individual streaks of those colors forming the dark purple.

"There's no doubt of his feelings, and Connor's are equally strong. His affection for you glows brightly, a sunny yellow with streaks of orange, indicating happiness." My mouth quirked up in a smile at the thought. I could believe Connor's aura would resemble perpetual sunshine.

"You need to stop worrying. You've already won her heart. Trust that love always finds a way." Grannie's admonishment caught our attention, and we watched Connor flush under her gaze. He nodded, and I knew he'd asked her if Jules would accept his proposal. I'd told him she wanted to be proposed to as they jumped out of a plane skydiving, and after several minutes of hyperventilating, he'd managed to choke out an okay.

As amusing as it would have been, I knew she'd kill me if he actually did it, so I told him the truth. I described the image I'd seen of a fairytale proposal, surrounded by everyone she loved, and by the time I finished, he no longer wanted to kill me for trying to get him to skydive. At least, until I told him Jake knew he planned to propose, and he'd better ask his permission.

"And you," she turned her knowing gaze to Jake, capturing him. "You worry so much over her, fearing things you can't fight will take her from you." She stroked his cheek. "Your fear is not unfounded, but you must understand your own strength. You make her strong enough to fight. You make her strong. Have faith. It will stand you in good stead, child, for there will come a day when your voice is the only tie she has left to this world and without it …."

She shook her head, and worry tightened Jake's face. She sighed, giving him an understanding smile. "She needs you, as you need her. Know that it's enough."

She stood up, and for the first time, I could see how old she was. Jake and Connor murmured their thanks and came over to us. We knew our time was up, but as I glanced at the sketches lining the walls, I knew we'd be back. Mysteries were here for us to solve.

"Addie." Her voice drew me to her as the others stepped out to the front room. "The door ... have you made a decision?"

"I have no wish to know the future. There are too many possibilities, with no way of knowing how it will actually turn out." I knew she would understand what I meant, and her nod encouraged me to continue. "The door can stay shut. I won't be opening it." She grasped my hand in hers, her skin like paper, but her grip firm on mine.

"Sometimes, our best intentions aren't enough. Remember to listen." She touched my cheek gently as I nodded. Our eyes met, and I was afraid I understood her all too well. As much as I wished to keep the door closed, it had never been my decision to open it, and I feared what would happen when it eventually did.

"I have to go." She nodded, releasing me, and I walked to the curtain.

"Remember to listen, Addie. Follow it home." Her words were low, but I managed to catch them as I stepped out.

"You ready?" Jake's eyes crinkled at the corners as he smiled at me, and I remembered what Wade said about the colors flaring more brightly. I glanced at him, and he nodded, a small smile on his lips. I tucked myself into Jake, and smiled.

"I'll see you again soon, Wade."

Jake stuck his hand out and said, "Nice to meet you, man."

144

"You too." He shook both their hands, and Connor gave a last glance around.

"Cool place you have here," he smiled. "I have a feeling we'll be meeting again."

We piled into the Camaro, and Connor twisted around to look at me.

"Are we skipping class?" He wiggled his eyebrows at me, and I laughed.

"No. One of my professors decided to schedule an exam right before the holiday." I mock-frowned, my high at seeing the girls saved not destroyed in the least by the thought of an exam.

"That sucks. You deserve a day off for saving the day."

"Uh huh. Afraid real life doesn't work that way, Con."

"Ain't that the truth."

I met Jake's eyes in the rearview mirror.

"How long do you think the captain will wait?"

He shook his head.

"Not long."

We'd talked about what I'd seen from the captain before the rescue of the girls. The fact was, the captain actually thought they were handling too many cases, allowing the other guys in the unit to slack off. That was why he'd been reassigning cases from them. It had nothing to do with them, but the perception of workload.

Both guys had agreed to give the captain another chance, taking what I knew under consideration. The relationship would take time, but I had a feeling it would develop into a strong one. They all wanted the same things, after all. They just had different methods for achieving them. But we still owed him an explanation for how I'd known where the girls were.

"After class this afternoon." My nod was miniscule, but he caught it. "I'll meet with him then."

"And?"

"Tell him the truth." I took a deep breath. "I think it's for the best. I can convince him, and maybe it'll help him understand." Understand Jake and Connor's ability to solve cases was my thought, so maybe it would ease the captain's suspicions.

"You sure, Addie?" Connor reached back, gripping my hand, since Jake was driving. He thought I was making the right choice, but didn't want me to do anything I wasn't willing to do. They knew how difficult it was for me to explain my ability to others.

"Yeah. I am."

"Okay."

We pulled up outside the building where my first class was. I shook my head.

"So no more babysitters when I get out of class?"

"Nope. We got the bad guys, and they're singing like canaries. We have APBs out to pick up the others who weren't there when we rescued the girls."

"Doesn't mean you don't need to be careful, though." Jake's eyes met mine, his face serious. "And we'll pick you up after your last class to bring you to the precinct for the meeting with the captain."

I nodded, knowing I could drive myself, but wanting their support when I faced the captain. I leaned over, giving Jake a quick kiss on the lips.

"Yuck, why do you subject me to this?" Connor moaned dramatically, and I bussed him on the cheek.

"I love you too, Connie baby." I ruffled his hair and shot out of the car hearing him cry, "Hey."

I laughed and waved my hand at them before slipping through the door. Carly was directly on the other side, waiting for me.

"I was keeping watch."

146

"There is so nothing creepy about that."

She huffed and rolled her eyes tugging me to the corner.

"So ... it's over?"

I swayed, the darkness swirling under our feet as I fought to keep myself from going under.

"Addie!" Carly snapped her fingers under my nose. "Earth to Addie."

I blinked, steadying, as the dark receded from us.

"Are you all right?" She was concerned, and now so was I. It wasn't over. We'd missed something. I didn't know what, but the darkness indicated danger, and looking at Carly, I was reminded of my flash showing her injured.

"I'm fine." I managed a smile, and tucked my arm into hers. "Now, we have an exam to ace."

An hour later, I was waiting in the hall for her, having finished the exam first. It was odd standing there with no babysitter. For the first time, I missed them and the peace of mind their presence gave me. The echoing darkness that had come with Carly's question was more terrifying to me than any bad guy. It hinted at the unknown, the absence of everything, and the thought chilled me.

Carly burst through the door, startling me.

"Did I pass?" Her face was haggard, and her backpack slipped down her arm, but she gave me a hopeful look. My wide grin must have given her the answer she wanted, because she proceeded to fist pump down the hall singing 'We are the Champions.' I shook my head and followed her, unwilling to ruin her good mood with my own dark thoughts.

She came to a halt outside the door, looking around like she just realized something. I waited, shoving my hands into the pockets of my hoodie. My fingers bumped into something, and as I felt it, I realized my stun gun was in my pocket. I wrapped my fingers around it, feeling slightly more protected. Maybe I couldn't stop the darkness from coming, but I could fight against a physical foe.

"No bodyguards," Carly said in wonder. "So weird."

She shot me a playful look, "We can go off campus for lunch."

"You're a wild one," I laughed, her euphoric mood rubbing off on me. Jake would come after my last class. We would talk to the captain, and I would explain this lingering feeling of danger. Together, we could figure out what it was and stop it. For now, food was in order.

"Let's go to Acme's. I'm in the mood for oysters."

"Yay! That's what I was thinking too," Carly grinned, and we headed to her car.

"How's everything with Danny?" I questioned her, our conversation with Jules feeling like it was days ago, instead of just yesterday.

"Eh."

"Eh? Really? This from the girl that gushed over how your souls spoke to one another?"

"I know, and they do. But I don't know. He runs hot and cold."

"He likes you. Trust me, I know that much."

"I believe you, but he's been withdrawn. Yesterday, he was super distracted, and I don't know what's going on with him. I ask if everything is okay, and he says it's fine. But it's not."

She squeezed into a tiny parking spot behind the restaurant, one of the only spaces left, since we'd managed to arrive in the middle of the lunch rush.

"Ugh, their parking sucks."

"They're popular."

"I hate parking out here though. It's isolated."

"We'll be fine. I'm sure there will be plenty of people around when we leave."

We hopped out of the car, and I continued my line of questioning.

"Do you want to be with Danny?"

"Yes. But it takes two people to make a relationship. I want what you and Jake have; what Connor and Jules have. And for a minute, I thought Danny was stepping up. He asked me out, and we had a great time. It seemed like things were looking up."

"But? What happened?"

"He gets calls and won't tell me who they're from. I'm not trying to pry, but he's secretive about it. And he straight stood me up for a coffee date yesterday. You were out saving the world with your boyfriend, and mine was standing me up."

"That's not cool." I didn't mention it, but it also didn't sound like Danny. He'd been attentive when we were training at the gym, and I'd noticed a definite change in him after he reconnected with his parents.

"He apologized. Said it was work, and he couldn't get to the phone to let me know. And okay, I can accept that. But he's distracted and more brooding than normal."

"I didn't think that was possible."

She gave me a narrow glare, and I shrugged. It was true. His picture should be next to the definition of brood in the dictionary. However, if anyone would know the difference in his brooding level, it would be Carly. She'd been studying him for months, and I had to wonder what would be causing his distraction now.

The server interrupted my thoughts as she brought us to a tiny table in the back. The place was packed, but we managed to get our order in.

"Oysters Bienville."

"Rockefeller for me."

"Oh, and a dozen raw."

"Please."

"Thank you."

After getting our food, our conversation turned to the exam we'd just finished, and my morning meeting with Wade and his Grannie.

"So, she gave a reading to Jake and Connor? That is so cool. I wonder if she'll do one for me?"

"I have a feeling she will." I smiled at the thought, picturing Carly and Grannie doing a reading, especially after she'd accused them of being fakes when she'd met them.

"Are we ready to do our presentation next week?" Our criminal justice paper was due when we came back from break.

"Yes." She gave me a questioning look. "We are going to keep the paper the same? Exposing Fraudulent Psychics and Their Effects on Society?"

"Yes." I agreed. The topic still made me uncomfortable. I was some version of a psychic, and our paper felt like a witch hunt. I knew there were plenty of fraudsters duping people out of their money, but was our report negating the effects of people like myself and Wade?

"I have an idea about it." She held up her hand. "Now, don't shoot me. I was thinking we should change it just a little. Maybe add a piece about psychics working for the police department. A sort of counter-argument to our presentation. The benefits of having psychics in our midst."

"I think you just like to argue." A smile snuck out, even as I tried to contain it. We'd been friends a long time, and the fact that she was willing to do additional work, because of my hang up with our topic, proved what an incredible friend she was.

"Maybe I do, but I also know that for the dozen frauds we found there was a real one, and he saved lives. Just like you do. And we need to show that. Our world isn't cut and dry, and true psychics face ridicule and disbelief when they try to help, and that needs to change."

"You are pretty darn amazing yourself," I told her as I looked around. "What time is it?" The restaurant had emptied while we were talking, and I had a feeling we were going to be late.

"It's almost two. We're gonna be late for class."

"I can't believe I didn't notice."

We paid the check and dashed out. The parking lot was practically empty as we headed to Carly's car. I huddled into my jacket, as the wind cut through us. She fished her keys out, the car beeping as the locks disengaged. We were almost there, and in our rush, not paying attention to the area around us.

"Not so fast." My head jerked back, as someone had yanked on my ponytail. I reacted instinctively, spinning around to hook my attacker's leg and drop him. He anticipated my move, dodging, and I heard Carly scream. It distracted me as I spun around to see where she was.

The scene in front of me would be one I would never forget, as I watched Danny hold a struggling Carly, his hand over her mouth to stop her scream. The sight froze me for a second too long, giving my attacker the opportunity to knock me out.

I woke up to the taste of blood in my mouth, the pounding in my head matching the rocking motion I felt. The combination made me queasy as I attempted to sit up.

"Addie. Addie. Are you okay?" I started to nod, but the pain the motion caused stopped me. I waited for the dizziness to end before focusing on Carly. She was propped against the wall, her hair tangled around her face, and her hands and feet were tied together.

"I'm okay," I answered belatedly, noticing my own hands and feet were tied. The rocking led me to believe we were on a boat, but it wasn't dark, and they hadn't gagged or blindfolded us, so I wasn't sure if they were the same people that had taken the other five girls.

A thought niggled at me, something I'd seen, and as I remembered, I gazed at Carly in horror.

"Did you see who took us?"

She nodded frantically, but didn't look nearly as horrified as I felt, so I thought I must be mistaken. There was no way I'd seen Danny help kidnap us.

"I didn't recognize the guy who grabbed you. I never saw the guy that had me. He dropped a hood over my head, and they shoved us in a car." She frowned, her eyes red from suppressed tears. "This is why I hate that stupid parking lot. People can kidnap you."

Her words made me smile faintly, because even in the midst of a truly horrific situation, Carly could say something to make me smile. I scooted closer to her, the motion making me dizzy, as the throbbing in my head increased with each movement. It took what seemed like hours, but I finally made it to her side.

"Did you hear anything?" I asked, finding myself needing to lean against her and the wall, just to stay upright.

"The guy was ranting. Kept on and on about how you ruined his plans. He needed girls, and if he didn't have them, they would make him pay. I don't know why he blames you. The cops rescued the girls. He shouldn't have known anything about you."

"Ask me," I muttered, the throbbing in my head growing worse and forcing me to close my eyes.

"Addie, stay awake."

I pried my eyes open. "I'm awake. Light hurts my eyes. Ask me."

"Are you sure? You don't look so good."

My face was pasty white, blood trickling from my lip where he'd hit me, and I could see why she thought I wasn't up to it.

"We have to know. Information is our only advantage, right now." The dizziness made it easy for me to believe I was wrong about Danny. He couldn't have been the one to kidnap us, but my thoughts were inescapable. He'd been distant. He worked at the shipyard. He'd hauled the dead kidnapper out of the river. And the most damning of all … I knew he was the one who would hurt Carly.

But as my eyes skimmed over her, there were no marks on her. She hadn't been physically hurt while I was out cold.

"How did the crazy guy who kidnapped us know you were the one to tip the police?"

"Dirty snitch," I groaned, picturing the moment I'd told the captain I was the reliable source. There had been officers everywhere, but I hadn't noticed there'd also been a guy in handcuffs. "Lenny. He was in the station, when the captain demanded to know who the source of the tip was. Are all Lenny's bad? You ever heard of a good Lenny? Seems like the name of a low down lying little snitch."

"Good alliteration, but you're worrying me now."

"How are we going to get out of here?"

Her question opened the door, the dark void beckoning me with answers … or oblivion. Either was acceptable at the moment, as my head continued to throb, and I doubted our ability to escape.

"Addie!" A sharp elbow to my side caused me to cry out, bringing me back to the moment. "I don't know what just happened, but no more questions." The fear on her face kept me from arguing, my own weakness making me wonder if I would be able to survive the darkness if it came back.

We sat there for hours, listening to the rumble of machines and echoing thuds as more containers were loaded in the distance, and we huddled for warmth. We'd been left in a shipping container. It was as cold as Danny said, and there was no point in screaming. They hadn't gagged us, because no one would hear us. The container must have already been loaded on the ship, and as the other sounds faded, I thought we were done. Once the ship was on the river and moving, it would be difficult, if not impossible, for Jake to find us.

Truthfully, I wasn't sure how he'd find us now. He would have known something was wrong when I didn't come out of class, but he thought the case was done. Would he suspect they hadn't gotten all of the traffickers, or something else? The thoughts drummed in time to the pounding of my head, the pain never abating as we waited.

I must have drifted off, because the screeching of metal on metal jolted my eyes open. The door of our prison slid open with a painful shriek, our captor strutting in as a woman stumbled behind him, crying.

"You have made my life extraordinarily difficult." He glared at me, so I smiled.

"Anytime."

"You think this is funny? Oh, no. You won't for long. Not when you see what I have planned for you." He kicked the woman crying on the ground. "Shut up!" He turned back to me. "I had a quota to meet, and thanks to you, I'll be short. But luckily, you will fulfill part of the agreement. They aren't too picky about looks."

"Lucky me," I drawled, forcing myself upright. Leaning showed weakness, and even though I didn't think I was capable of standing at the moment, much less fighting, I refused to appear as weak as I felt.

"Oh, they'll enjoy beating the spunk right out of you. Some buyers like to break them."

"You're the missing link. I knew you were out there, but I missed it. My bad." I shook my finger at him, my tied hands meaning I shook my whole hand, but he got the point.

"Dan. Get in here and shut this bitch up."

"What? Don't want to do your own dirty work?" I taunted him, already knowing who Dan would be and wanting to spare Carly the sight of him.

He walked in, his face expressionless, his black eyes as dark as the void I feared so much. I heard Carly cry behind me, "No." I glared at him, hoping against hope, it wasn't what I thought, that he was here to save us. Anything, but that he was part of this, that I'd known he would hurt her, but wanting to believe my own interpretation of his feelings for Carly, instead of the truth.

Carly lunged forward, managing to get to her knees, even with her feet tied.

"No, no, no. This isn't you. Dan ...." He walked forward, the blow casual as he backhanded her, slamming her head against the wall, blood streaming from her nose.

"You bastard!" I screamed as the reality of my vision appeared in front of me. He spun around, looking at me now. The absolute lack of emotion on his face made me wonder how I could have been so mistaken, if I'd somehow misjudged my ability, because there was no way the Danny who'd admitted his feelings was the same man in front of me.

The crazy psycho started laughing and clapping his hands, as if he was at the show.

"Ah, I'm feeling better already. You ruined my plans, you stupid meddling bitch. If you weren't worth more to me alive, I'd kill you now, just for the sheer aggravation you've caused me." He glanced at Danny, "Shut her up. We need to go. We're short a girl, and I'm not showing up at the meeting without something else to pacify them."

Danny crouched down in front of me, a smirk forming on his face as I backed up, not wanting any part of me to touch him.

"Hurry up!" The little man hopped up and down, his impatience clear. "We have a meeting to go to."

"Stay away from me," I growled, my own pain forgotten as I saw the broken look on Carly's face as she watched Danny.

"You think I won't kill you?" he taunted, a smile spreading across his face, at the sight of the horror on mine.

"BASTARD!" I screamed, spitting at him, even as his fist slammed into my face, sending me spinning into the dark void his question had opened.

Chapter Fourteen

I drifted, the dark void which had terrified me, now comforting. There was no pain here. No fear. Worry couldn't even penetrate the darkness I found myself in. Occasional flickers of light would draw my attention, but they moved so quickly, I couldn't determine what they were.

"Addie."

My head turned toward the sound of my name, but it was so faint, and the darkness had become familiar, so I ignored it. Another flicker, this one containing an image, drew me toward it.

"Addie."

The voice was persistent, but the flickering image had my attention, as I saw myself in it. I drifted closer, my will seeming to slow the image, so I could watch it like a movie playing in front of me.

"Addie, push." He held my hand, a loving smile on his face.

"I AM." My body bent forward as a contraction came again.

"Not much more," the doctor encouraged, and even though the pain felt like it was going to tear me in two, I bore it, knowing why I did it. The bitch retracted her claws, and I collapsed back, panting, wondering why the hell I didn't go with an epidural.

Oh yeah, my fear of needles.

That was dumb of me.

"You're doing great." He wiped my face, and I managed a smile. His eyes were green at the moment; they always were when they were filled with emotion. He was proud of me. That much was clear, from the expression on his face. I arched up again, as the pain came back, feeling like claws were wrapping around my torso and squeezing the shit out of me.

"Push. One good push, and we'll have a baby." Those words were enough to make me push harder than I'd ever pushed in my life.

I felt a rush between my legs and the words, "It's a boy!"

I collapsed back on the bed, tears seeping from the corners of my eyes. Jake gazed down at me, leaning over, and cupping my cheek. "You did good."

"Daddy, you want to cut the cord?" Jake glanced back at the doctor, and then nodded over at Connor.

"Go ahead." I smiled at the sight of Connor's shaking hands as he cut the last physical tie of his son to me. Jake kissed me, whispering, "You never cease to amaze me with your strength."

As they cleaned up the baby boy, Jules and Connor hovered nearby, watching. Once the nurse had him clean and swaddled, she handed him to Jules.

"Congratulations." Tears ran down her face as she stared at the tiny baby created by her and Connor, and carried by me. I'd never thought the first baby I carried wouldn't even be mine, but life had a funny way of working out.

"Addie." The voice was a little louder now, the desperation in it tugging at me, and the image in front of me disappeared, zooming into the void with the others. The vision I'd seen made me happy though, and I wanted to see more.

I reached out eagerly, slowing another image. It was my graduation from college, a happy smile on my face as I caught my mom's eyes in the audience. But as I touched the image, it flipped. I was still graduating, but there were no happy smiles, no one waiting in the audience to watch me accept my diploma. My hand drew back, the double sided image spinning away.

The darkness didn't feel as comforting now.

"Listen." This time the word was an echo of a memory, but another image caught my eye and I seized it, the sensation of falling overtaking me.

"Momma."

"Yes?" I replied, ruffling the caramel waves on his head. He was a miniature version of Jake, not one shred of me in him anywhere. I shook my head, smiling at the serious expression on his face. "What has you looking so serious?"

His face became even more upset, and I crouched down to his level. He'd started preschool a few weeks before, and he seemed like he was enjoying it. His cousin, Matthew, had told him all about it, and he'd been eager to go, but he'd been quiet since I'd picked him up today.

"Maggie had a bruise on her arm today," he told me, pointing to his forearm. "Right here, and it was big. But you couldn't see it, cause of her shirt." I nodded, worried about where this was going, but needing him to tell me. "The teacher asked her where she got the bruise and she told her she fell down." He peered at me, his hazel eyes green. "She didn't fall. Her mommy grabbed her arm and shook her. That's why she had a bruise."

I ran my hands up and down his arms, comforting him and warming my suddenly cold hands. "Did Maggie tell you that's how she got her bruise?" I asked him carefully, already suspecting he would see more in my question.

He shook his head. "No, I knowed it. Like you."

I closed my eyes briefly. The idea that a child of mine could inherit my gift had crossed my mind, but I'd never known for sure if it was genetic, if I'd inherited it from someone.

"It's not easy, but we can help Maggie, because you can see the truth." I told him, brushing back the hair that fell into his eyes. "I think you need a haircut."

"Like Daddy's?" He wanted his hair to be cut like Jake's, and I nodded, standing up with the knowledge our son had inherited at least one thing from me.

"Addie, you need to come back. Baby, I love you. Addie."

The voice was louder, forcing me to listen. I turned back, wanting a last glimpse of our son, but the image was gone.

My thoughts swirled, the images I'd seen reminding me of my life, the darkness becoming oppressive, instead of comforting. The voice calling my name came again, and I pushed toward it, knowing I needed to answer it.

Another image drifted by, this one an image from my past, my curiosity compelling me closer, as I saw my mom holding me as a baby.

My mom was much younger, and talking to a man that was vaguely familiar.

"I'm not a perfect man, but I love you both."

"You can't keep a job. You spent the rent money." She shifted, and the baby girl on her hip watched them argue. "What do you expect me to do? I can't take care of you and Addie. Someone has to be the adult." She shook her head. "And obviously it's not going to be you. You say you love us, but enough to work hard and support a family? Do you even want to be here?"

Her question made my younger self cry, and she shushed her, kissing her head to comfort her as I watched, connecting dots. She didn't see the pain on the man's face, as he heard what I'd heard. My mom didn't want him there. He'd made life hard for us, and she was tired of supporting a man that couldn't give her what they needed. She didn't love him, not like she loved the baby girl in her arms.

"You've answered your own question, Diane. I'm not a perfect man, not by any means, but I can do the right thing, on occasion."

160

He walked away as tears slipped from her eyes, a mixture of pain and relief reflected on her face.

"Something will happen here, and we have to figure it out!"

The shout drew me to another image, and as much as I wanted to resist, it drew me in.

Wade stood there, a harsh expression on his face as he waved a drawing at me.

"I don't know what will happen." My exasperation was clear. Wade had stormed in with a sketch in his hand, needing me to tell him what had happened at the place he'd drawn. I didn't have an answer for him, but he wasn't accepting it.

"But something will." He was determined, and I lifted my hands helplessly. "We can go there, look around, see if there's a clue. Maybe one of us will have a vision."

"Wade," I paused, understanding his pain. There was nothing quite like the feeling of losing someone you loved, and he was desperate to feel the hole his Grannie's passing had left. It didn't help that she'd been the only family he had.

"Don't say it." He turned away, shaking his head impatiently. "I keep dreaming of this place. I've sketched it dozens of times. Something about this place … it's important. I'm not avoiding my feelings. I'm doing what she would have wanted. What you used to want to do, until you lost your ability."

"I haven't lost it."

"Really? Because it sure seems like you have."

The scene blinked away, but I still felt the fear. The fear I'd felt when he'd said what everyone else had been afraid to say, when he said it out loud. Lost my ability. The thought made me feel as if a limb had been torn from me, a piece of me gone, and I wondered if this was my future.

161

"Addie. I'm scared now. It's been too long. The doctors don't understand. It doesn't make sense. I know you can hear me. But you're not listening. Addie. Wake up. Addie."

The words cut through my fear, tugging at me, and I wanted to answer him. He was waiting for me, and I'd promised him. I fought, determined to follow his voice this time. A pinpoint of light became my guide as I struggled against the darkness holding me.

An image raced toward me. Any attempt to avoid it was pointless, as it hit me, sending me tumbling into another scene, one I didn't want to see.

I stood in what appeared to be a park, the scent of freshly mown grass tickling my nose. A gravel path wound under my feet, encouraging me to follow it. I walked for a distance leaving the path, my head ducking under a low limb instinctively, as if I'd done it many times before.

"Addie." My head turned at the sound of my name being called, but no one was there. Suddenly, I could see what I hadn't seen earlier, rows and rows of markers dotting the grass. I turned, finding where my steps had taken me, and felt myself fall as my legs gave out. The sight in front of me was impossible. I shook my head, earlier visions trickling through my mind. There was no way, absolutely not—this was not my future. My sobs choked me, each vision racing through my mind as I stared at the end, the finality of us.

"Listen. Follow it home."

"Addie. Addie. I'm not giving up."

"They're possibilities, Addie."

I stared up at her, not understanding how she could be standing with me in this place.

"Grannie."

She smiled, the sight familiar and comforting.

"I warned you about the door."

I nodded, inexplicably ashamed of failing her. "Don't be ashamed. You haven't failed me. I warned you, but sometimes our best intentions aren't enough."

I blinked at her in shock, as she seemed to read my mind.

She smiled, understanding.

"A gift of the moment, child."

I nodded, my gaze drawn back to the tombstone in front of me, seeing my name etched into the stone.

"Am I dying then?" I wondered if this place would be where I died, or if everything I'd just seen was nothing more than an illusion, and I was already dead.

"I don't know. That's up to you." She sat down on my tombstone, patting it gently. "Possibilities. Everything you've seen here is nothing but a possibility. The future is what you make it."

Her question broke through the fear I felt, releasing a ray of hope, and giving me strength. If what she said was true, then I'd seen what my life could be, the future we could all have. I gazed up at her, my eyes hopeful.

"You can change it, but you have to get up." She glanced around, and as I looked up, I could see the sky wasn't blue, but instead I saw the black void, images flickering like stars. "This place is dangerous, but sometimes we have to see what the future holds, so we can know what is important. What's worth fighting for, even in the darkest of hours."

"Addie." My head jerked toward the voice, my eyes focusing on a light brighter than the images.

"Follow it home, Addie."

I glanced at her one last time, her face as unlined as a child's, and she began to fade, her smile one I would never forget.

163

"Tell Wade I love him."

"ADDIE!"

"ADDIE!"

The light grew with the sound of my name being called, until it finally blinded me, as my eyes blinked open.

Chapter Fifteen

His face was the first thing I saw, and the most welcome one.

"Jake." My voice was raspy with disuse, my throat painfully dry, and I felt weak as a kitten as I tried to reach up to him.

"Shh, you've been out for a bit." He leaned down to kiss me, careful not to hurt me, and I did hurt. The realization came over me as I became aware of my body. The darkness had captured my mind, leaving me weightless, and hiding the fact that I was bruised.

"What happened?"

"A lot. But I need to get the doctor and your mom."

He swayed as he straightened, and I could see the shadows under his hollowed eyes. He was exhausted and drained, and I wondered how long I'd been out of it. It didn't look as if he'd left my side.

"Ms. Michaels," he called out the door, and I heard her quick footsteps. She came around the door, the relief on her face overwhelming.

"Addie!" she cried, running to my bed. She hugged me, the movement sending pain through my head, but it didn't matter. We both needed the hug. "You've got to stop doing this. I can't keep getting calls that you're in the hospital, because of some police thing. What were you thinking?" Her question drifted through me, the answer gone before I could grab it.

"I love you," I answered her, knowing she needed to hear it.

"I'm going to get the doctor." I heard him step out, giving us privacy, and my mom frowned at the door where he'd been.

"He's the reason you're in here." Her mouth was tight, anger lacing her words, and I shook my head.

"No, he's not. Trust me. It's just as much my fault." She glared, unwilling to let her anger go, and I took her hand. "So much I need to tell you."

"You need to get well. You had a concussion from being hit in the face. You've been in a coma, and the doctors couldn't figure out why."

A knock on the door interrupted us, and the doctor stepped in.

"I'm glad to see those eyes open. You had us worried."

He asked me questions, going through a list of things to check that I was all there. My eyes were heavy, exhaustion pulling at me, because even though it appeared I'd been asleep for days, it felt like I hadn't slept at all.

"Sleep. Heal," Mom murmured to me, as the need for sleep overtook my resistance.

"We'll be here." Jake smiled encouragingly, and I wanted to tell them both to get some sleep as well, but couldn't form the words as sleep overtook me.

It was dark when I opened my eyes again, and fear jolted me. The beeping sounds of the machines hooked to me helped me to remember where I was and slow the racing of my heart, as I realized it was only the room that was dark, and I wasn't trapped in the black void any longer. A void I'd had reason to fear, one that had given answers, while raising new questions.

"Are you awake?"

I smiled at the voice, glad he was here.

"Yeah. Where are they?"

"Your mom went home to check on your grandfather and hopefully to get some sleep. Jake is sleeping on the lumpy-ass sofa they call a pullout bed."

"And you?"

"Reporting for guard duty."

166

My breath huffed out in a small laugh, and I saw the white of his teeth as he grinned.

"You gave us a scare. He hasn't left your side. Talking to you nonstop. Determined you would wake up, even as the doctors scratched their heads over your coma."

"How long?"

"Three days."

"What day is it?"

"Tuesday. You've been out since Friday."

A thought wriggled into my brain, causing me to smile.

"Happy Birthday."

He chuckled, his hand warm around mine.

"Trust you to be the first person to wish me happy birthday in years, and you just woke up from a coma."

"It wasn't a coma. I'm not sure I was asleep," I whispered, my voice cracking as I attempted to use it. He handed me a cup, the straw sliding as I caught it with my lips. I sucked, the cool water easing the ache.

"The door?"

"Jake told you."

"Yeah, kinda pissed me off you didn't tell me."

"I didn't want to worry you."

"Yeah, not really a good enough answer."

"I'm sorry. Truly."

"Yeah, guess I shouldn't be fussing while you're lying in a hospital bed."

"Ha, I would expect nothing less from you." He squeezed my hand extra tight, and I gave a small groan. "What happened?"

"That's a long story."

"I'm not going anywhere."

"True." He took a deep breath. "We'd thought we'd gotten all the bad guys, had APBs on the ones who weren't there, but we missed one. The one that came after you."

I nodded, remembering the little psycho man.

"He kidnapped you and Carly, and brought you to the ship that was supposed to take the kidnapped girls overseas. We rescued them in the nick of time, by the way. We'd messed up his plan, so that's why he went after you, and Carly just happened to be there."

"Is she okay?"

I felt his pause.

"She'll be okay. Physically, she's fine, but emotionally … I think she's going to need time. A lot happened."

"Danny." I knew that betrayal would be difficult to look past. He'd hurt her physically and emotionally. She'd watched him come at me, after hitting her. It wouldn't be easy to live with that.

"He was doing his job."

"I know. He made it a point to ask me a question. I saw the truth even as he knocked me out. But Carly didn't know."

"Yeah, and he's beating himself up over both of you. He didn't want any of that to happen. But he didn't have a choice. They didn't trust him and only used him, once we'd arrested half their damn goonies."

"He was Jake's backup plan."

"Yep. And it's a damn good thing, even though I could kick his ass for hiding it from me and you."

"Hidden lies," I whispered, knowing he'd had to be very careful to keep his plan from me. It seemed redundant. A lie, by its nature, was something to be kept hidden, but that was a difficult task around me. He'd managed it, though.

"He wanted a guy on the inside. In case you couldn't find anything. Plus, he was scared, scared of how terrified you were.

The door, your reaction to the questions about the girls. It all had him pushing to make sure he had his bases covered."

"I'm not mad. He was right. If Danny hadn't been there …."

"Yeah, I know. Trust me, the thought has haunted me, since we realized you were taken." He cleared his throat. "Danny let us know as soon the guy kidnapped y'all. But we couldn't move too soon."

"There was a meeting," I said, remembering the conversation between Danny and the psycho.

"Yep. An important meeting that we invited ourselves too."

I could see his face more clearly now, my eyes adjusted to the darkness, ambient light seeping in from the hallway. His smile was wicked and a tad bit smug.

"We caught a lot of very bad guys at that meeting."

"Good. I'm glad my kidnapping and getting beat up served a purpose."

He chuckled, rubbing my hand with his thumb.

"It did. You do seem to have a talent for catching bad guys, even accidentally."

"Accident? It was all part of my grand plan to save the world."

"I can see that happening." He hesitated, and I nudged his hand.

"Finish."

"You're going to need to talk to the captain. Carly told us about Lenny and the captain is blaming himself. He pushed you to reveal yourself and then you were kidnapped. He has a lot of questions and guilt."

"Sounds like I need to talk to a lot of people."

"What did you see, Addie?"

His question forced a heavy sigh from me.

"Too much."

"Want to talk about it?"

"Not really."

"We're here. All of us. We want to be here. And we'll listen."

"I know. I love you for it."

"I should leave you to rest."

"No, stay please." I squeezed his hand, not wanting to be left alone. The darkness had scared me, and if my suspicions were true, Grannie was gone. Tears seeped down my cheeks at the thought of her loss, of Wade's loss.

"Was what you saw so bad then?" he whispered, catching sight of my tears. I shook my head, remembering the sight of his shaking hands as he cut the umbilical cord. A trembling smile broke through my sorrow.

"I saw your son being born."

A shocked happiness crossed his face, and he kissed the back of my hand. He leaned his elbows on the bed, smiling as he shook his head at me.

"How?"

He was asking how I knew, but also how it would happen. I wasn't sure I was ready to tell him the how of any of it. I wasn't certain what the darkness had been or why it had opened in my mind, but Grannie's words echoed. There would be troubles ahead, and I would need to hold tight to the joy, to the visions of what the future could be, if I fought for it.

"I'm not sure I can explain, but trust me. He'll be born. I promise you that."

The next morning, I woke up to see Carly sitting next to my bed, both of her eyes bruised and a bandage on her nose.

I teared up, my emotions all over the place as I told her, "I'm sorry. It was my fault you were taken."

"No, it wasn't. It was the bad guy. Wrong place, wrong time. Now stop crying, or you'll set me off. I've cried enough the last few days, wondering if you'd wake up. I'd rather not cry, now that you have."

A laugh choked me, but it managed to help me control the tears.

"Are you okay?"

She nodded, her eyes uncertain, but resolute.

"Yes. I will be."

"And Danny?"

The mask broke, and I could see the pain she'd been trying to hide, her lips white as she pressed them together.

"He did what he had to, and I understand that. My head understands that." She looked at me, her eyes watery. "My heart isn't so sure. There's a distance now, that wasn't there. I don't know what to do now. I don't know." Her words broke off, her pain piercing me.

"It'll be okay. You'll figure it out, and I'll be here for you while you do," I promised her, reaching for her hand. She gripped my hand, shaking her head.

"You're the one in the hospital bed, and here I am crying over a boy."

"Pretty sure he doesn't qualify as a boy, and that's what friends do." She smiled at my words, and I squeezed her hand. "I saw the truth when he asked me the last question. He was trying to keep us safe. Remember that."

She nodded. "I'm trying, and I know he was."

"But?"

"I'm scared of him."

Her fingers tightened around mine at the admission, and I knew then, it would take a long time for Carly to rebuild the trust she had in Danny. Fear wasn't any easy thing to overcome, and it didn't care about logic.

"I don't want to be afraid. I don't, but it's how I feel when I'm near him or think about him. The terror of that room, being hit, watching you collapse and not wake up. It's all tied to him for me."

"We'll get through this together. We'll figure it out. You're the most compassionate and forgiving person I know, and this is a bump in the road."

"I'm glad you're awake," she sniffed. "I didn't want to have to give the criminal justice presentation alone."

I laughed, glad she was here to remind me I was alive for a reason. The visions I'd had while trapped in my own mind were etched inside of me. The last one threatened to drag me under, anytime my thoughts went near it. Seeing the name on the tombstone had caused my worst nightmare to become my reality. If it hadn't been for Grannie, I might have stayed there forever, too lost to pull myself out.

"Carly," I said, catching her attention, and she glanced at me curiously. "Can you get a hold of Wade for me? I have a message for him."

"Okay. I can do that."

"Ladies."

We both looked up at the door to see Danny standing there, uncomfortably. Carly stood up.

"I'm gonna go. I'll find Wade for you." She bobbed her head and skirted around Danny. He held out a hand toward her, the pain on his face difficult for me to witness.

"I'm so sorry. I truly am. I know words aren't enough."

She paused, not making eye contact, her body stiff as she leaned away from him.

172

"I need time."

She slipped out the door, practically running down the hall. Danny stood there watching her, his hand still raised. I blinked back tears of my own, the sight breaking my heart. Danny had lost so much, and as understandable as Carly's fear was, I cursed the situation. If she hadn't been with me, she would have been safe, and never had to feel the fear she was currently feeling, a fear that was worse, because it had once been affection.

He lowered his hand, clearing his throat as he peered at me. He continued to hover by the door, not coming in, so I beckoned him closer.

"Do you hate me?" His own self-loathing washed over me, a jumble of emotions disappearing as quickly as they arrived.

"No, not at all." He perched on the chair Carly had just vacated, gazing at me with the saddest puppy eyes I'd ever seen, which was singularly impressive, because I thought Connor had long ago mastered the look. "Not as much as you hate yourself. Which, by the way, is pointless. You did what you had to do, and you saved our lives in the process."

"I put you in a coma!" He burst out, his entire body in motion as he pushed himself up and began pacing. "I blackened both of Carly's eyes and busted her nose. I taunted you. And gave you a concussion."

"I actually think the master sociopath who originally took me gave me the concussion, to be honest." My correction didn't seem to help matters, as he continued to beat himself up over everything.

"I should have gotten Jake in there sooner. Got y'all out before that could happen. Killed the guy, anything."

"Danny."

He kept going, muttering so fast, I couldn't make out the words.

"Danny," I huffed, pulling myself up. "Don't make me get out of this bed."

He stopped, and seeing me struggle with the stupid bedsheets someone had felt the need to tuck around me, he came to help.

"I don't think you should get out of the bed."

"Then quit pacing around my room blaming yourself for saving us." I stopped trying to untwist the sheets from my legs and studied him. "You are not responsible for everything. You did the best you could with what you knew. I'm not mad. And Carly …"

His look was hopeless, and I decided not to tell him she feared him. My track record with not telling people things was not so good, but I didn't think he needed to feel any worse at the moment.

"You love her, and Danny, love ain't easy. Sometimes, it requires a fight, and you don't seem like the type to give up. So don't."

Resolve filled him as he nodded at me. The busted knuckles on his right hand caught my attention as he touched my arm. I placed my hand over them, seeing him frown and attempt to curl them out of sight.

"I'm sorry you got hurt." He froze, looking at me with astonished eyes. His t-shirt was too thin under the leather jacket; his jeans were stained with grease; and he'd recently buzzed his hair. He looked intimidating as hell, but underneath it, I could see what Carly had seen: a little boy lost to the violence he'd been forced to commit. A man whose heart was in the right place. "You had to do something you didn't want to do to protect us. You're hurting, and I'm sorry for that."

I squeezed his hand and let go, watching him step back as he gave me a confused nod. I caught sight of Jake in the door, watching us, and then Danny saw him.

"I'm going to go," he muttered, nodding at Jake before looking away. Jake grasped his hand, not letting him walk away. Danny paused, waiting for Jake to speak.

"I can't thank you enough for being there for my girl. Saving her. Truly, you don't know how grateful I am."

He pulled him into a hug, tapping him on the back. Danny was stiff at first, but eventually returned the hug.

"I'm glad she's okay." He glanced back at me then, a small smile on his lips as he nodded and left.

Jake sighed, his expression difficult to read as he crossed the room toward me.

"You know how many people I need to thank for you being here? It's crazy how many. I can't decide if you have nine lives or what."

"Twenty-seven."

He appeared puzzled for a second. Then his face cleared.

"And I'm sure you can give me their names too."

"If you want, but I think you already know."

He leaned down, pressing his lips against my temple, and tucked my hands into his.

"You have no idea how good it is to see your eyes open."

"Thanks to you." Staring at him I noticed his eyes were greener than I'd ever seen them.

"I truly thought I might lose you." He shook his head. "But I kept remembering your words. You knew it would be okay, because I could bring you back. Grannie told me my voice would be your only tie. So, I talked and didn't stop talking, until I saw those eyes open."

His voice was raspy as he sat down on the bed next to me.

"I heard you." He gazed at me, our hands tangled together as we spoke. "I heard you, and I followed you home."

175

He nodded, his eyes bright with emotion.

"There were visions … images … it was like a movie playing in my head. Different scenes. The future, the past, and things that hurt to think about. Grannie was there." I let out a shaky breath. "She helped me." Jake nodded, reaching up with our joined hands to swipe a tear from cheek. "I saw my grave."

His face froze in horror.

"No." He shook his head, denying my words. "You're alive. You made it. You can't die."

I shook my head, smiling.

"I'm not. At least not for a while. I think it was close, though. That's why Grannie was there. She knew I needed help getting out. She warned me about how dangerous that place was. I heard you, and I wanted to reach you, but it was as if you were too far away. And then … I wound up in a cemetery, sitting in front of a grave with my name on it."

"I'm so sorry you had to see that."

I nodded, remembering the horror of seeing my name etched in the stone, wondering if I was dead.

"She came then, and told me it didn't have to end that way. That I could choose to get up, listen to you, and follow you home." My smile was tremulous. "I got up." He brushed my cheek, tears glistening in his own eyes. "I saw a future with you. Things that need to be set right. The good we can do."

His eyes closed for a second, relief chasing away the fear from knowing how close to death I'd come. He stroked my jaw, pressing a light kiss against my temple and settled on the bed next to me.

"I think the door is gone."

Hope flared in his eyes as he cocked his head.

"I think Grannie shut it, when I came back to you. I don't feel it there anymore. Maybe I saw what I needed to see."

"I'm grateful to her. For helping you home and making sure you were safe."

He turned, laying down next to me, and I shifted to give him room. He wrapped his arms around me, and I tucked myself into him. My hand rested over his heart, the steady beat soothing me.

"Tell me about our future."

I smiled, thinking about the good things I saw. I ignored the visions I'd seen of my graduation, of Wade accusing me of losing my ability—those would be dealt with on another day.

"Our son will look like you, but he'll be like me."

My eyes were uncertain as they met his. He'd always accepted me, putting up with the craziness that accompanied my ability, but would he be okay with a son who also could do it?

"I can't wait to meet him." He rested his hand on my stomach, his thumb stroking gently. I peeked up at him, his expression one I'd never seen. It was a soft pride, mingled with love and hope. It made my heart ache as I stared at him, knowing he would be the father of our children.

"But first ..." His eyes shot to mine. "I'll need to give birth to your nephew."

His shock turned into a rolling laugh, and he tugged me toward him, squeezing gently.

"Why am I not surprised?"

He tilted my chin up, our lips brushing as he whispered, "I love you and our future children. I will fight for us every single day into eternity."

Chapter Sixteen

"It has to be perfect."

"Really? I just thought it had to be a diamond."

I slammed the car door a little harder than necessary, my frustration growing.

"I'm sorry. I'm nervous." He stood next to me in front of the jewelry store, reaching over for my hand. "Forgive me?"

One glance at him and I gave an exasperated sigh. Damn puppy eyes.

"Yes, but trust me when I say I know what she wants. Hello! Psychic girl."

"I know, but you've been a little on edge since the incident." That was how we'd come to refer to it. It wasn't really the kidnapping and beating, but the three-day coma he was referring to. He was right. I had been on edge.

It'd been over a month since we'd buried Grannie and I'd talked to him. He'd stared at me, the pain too new and raw to comprehend, and I knew I'd need to go see him soon. He was alone now, his Grannie the only family he'd had left. Her death had left a different kind of void in both of us. One caused by loss, and the other the absence of her love and understanding. She'd saved me from my own mind, closing the door permanently. I didn't know how she'd done it, only that she had, and I was grateful.

"I know I have."

He looked down at me, and I attempted a smile. "But today, we are ring shopping, and it has to be perfect." His own smile lit up his face, and mine felt more genuine. He threw his arm around me, squeezing me.

"You're the best, Addie."

"Trust me, I know."

We walked into the small shop tucked into a row of other stores in the downtown antique district. Connor had questioned me when I told him to come here for Jules' ring, but I'd insisted. We would find it here, the ring I'd pictured when she'd been asked about engagement rings. It wasn't your traditional ring, but Jules wasn't a traditional girl. She wanted something that represented them, and I knew we'd find it here.

"Welcome, how can I help you?"

"We're looking for engagement rings," Connor announced, reaching out to shake the gentleman's hand.

"Antique rings, to be precise."

"Of course, we have several to choose from. Congratulations."

"Thank you, but I haven't asked her yet. But I have it on good authority she'll say yes." The man squinted at us curiously, but I only smiled.

"Here is our collection of antique rings. We have several. Some are engagement rings, others dinner rings. We have diamonds, rubies, and emeralds." I scanned them, looking for the perfect ring.

"Do you see it?" Con whispered next to me, causing me to jump at his closeness.

"It would be easier if you didn't hover," I gritted out, poking him in the stomach. The man assisting us looked askance, his brow furrowing at our remarks. I gave him a bright smile and continued to look, while Connor wandered over to another display case. I frowned as I examined the rings. None of them were exactly right.

"Addie," Connor hissed, motioning me over. "Look at this one."

I wandered over to him, and seeing the ring he pointed out, I laughed.

"What? It might not be perfect, but you don't have to laugh," he grumbled, moving away from me, his hurt clear.

"No, Connor, I'm not laughing at you, but myself."

He glanced at me then, the assistant hovering behind the counter watching us.

"You found it. All by yourself. The perfect ring."

"Really?" His excitement was contagious, as he realized what I was saying. "I found it." He lifted me off my feet as he twirled me around the store. "I found it!"

He kissed my cheek, setting me down. "We found it." He turned to the man and proudly said, "That's the ring."

He blinked at us and withdrew the ring from the case.

"Would the miss like to try it on? So, we can get the correct size?"

"Oh, her fingers are way too big. She's practically got man hands."

I slapped his arm at the insult and told the man, "It'll need to be a size five."

He opened his mouth, hesitating, and then finally said, "Yes, ma'am."

I grinned and turned to Connor. "One perfect ring down, now on to the proposal. You have everything ready?"

"Yes. Everyone will be there. The weather should be perfect. And she'll be surprised, right? She doesn't suspect?"

I shook my head, knowing she didn't have a clue.

"You're in luck, sir. This ring is a size five."

"Somehow, I'm not surprised."

"It *is* the perfect ring."

The assistant boxed the ring and rang it up, announcing the total. Connor choked, looking back at me with raised eyebrows. I shrugged, mouthing, "You picked it."

He shuddered, handing the man his credit card.

"Addie."

"Yeah?"

"We'll need to stop by the gas station on the way home."

I laughed, looping my arm through his as we walked out.

"Can we make a stop first?'

"Sure."

I tugged him down the sidewalk, when he attempted to go to the car. "This way." We walked down the block, stopping in front of the psychic shop, where a sign proclaimed them closed, due to a death in the family.

"Addie, it doesn't look like he's here."

I gazed up at him questioningly, and he gave me a resigned look.

"Is anyone here?" he obliged me.

"Why, yes, they are."

I proceeded to pound on the door, until a rumpled Wade finally opened it.

"Addie. Of course."

I stepped in, forcing him to step back, and Connor wandered in behind me.

"I'm not in the mood for company," he told us quietly.

"I know, but that doesn't mean you don't need company." I pushed our way past the curtain into the backroom. As I glanced around, everything looked the same, except there was a new sketch on the wall, the same one Wade had texted me, the one that had saved the girls' lives.

"I saw things. Visions of the future. Grannie was there to save me from getting lost in them. Told me life needed to be lived, and I'd seen what I needed to see. She told me to tell you she loves you."

He avoided my eyes, his face pained.

"I'm going to keep coming back. I won't leave you here. I think we need each other." I waved my hand around the room at the sketches framed on the wall. "These visions need us."

He finally met my gaze.

"Maybe I don't care."

"But you do. We both do. And we can make it right." I bit my lip, needing to hear what I was about to say to him as much as he did. "We need to make it right, because we're the only ones who can. We see it, hear it, and know it for a reason, Wade. Don't close the shop. Don't walk away from who you are. I've been denying myself for a very long time. And you can't hide from yourself. Just so you know."

"You sound just like her when you say that."

"Thank you. I'll take that as a compliment."

He nodded, looking around again.

"How?"

"Well, it seems the police captain is open to consulting with psychics. It doesn't really pay a lot, but I think between the two of us, we could do a lot of good. I know a couple cops who are believers. They respect psychics."

"Really …. That's an interesting thought."

"Think it over. Call me when you're ready."

"And when will I be ready?"

"Tuesday."

"Till Tuesday then."

"I have a meeting with the captain. You should join us."

"Do I have a choice?"

"You always have a choice." Our eyes met, and I knew he understood me. "I'll see you then." A small smile lifted the corner of his mouth as we left, the doorbells jingling behind us.

"I still can't believe the captain is paying you as a consultant. You think he'll do the same for Wade?"

"Yep. Wouldn't have told him if I didn't think he would."

The captain's offer had taken us all by surprise. Once I'd been released from the hospital, I'd finally met with him. My explanation for knowing where the girls were and my assistance with Jake and Connor's other cases hadn't been dismissed as ridiculous.

Instead, he'd been curious about my ability, and after determining I wasn't lying, had offered me a consultant job. He felt if I was going to be assisting with cases, I should be paid. Like I'd told Wade, it wasn't much money and was on a case-by-case basis, but having a legitimate position on the force with Jake was worth more than the money. It felt like acceptance.

Connor stopped in front of my dorm, surprising me, because I hadn't even noticed the trip home.

"I'll see you tomorrow night."

"Yep, um, Connor?"

"Yeah?"

"We didn't stop by the gas station."

"Aw, shit. Get back in."

There was a light breeze causing the lanterns to sway, their flames flickering as dusk fell. I waited under the limb of a live oak, smoothing my dress. Everyone had gathered at the plantation house Connor had rented for the night, decorated in a rustic theme of candlelight and romance, night jasmine blooming as music played lightly in the darkness.

Connor stood confidently, the nerves that had haunted him all week gone as he waited for Jules to arrive. Natalie, John and their son, Tyler, stood next to me. Connor's parents were across the courtyard talking to Jake's parents. Carly chatted with Wade, and Danny stood quietly next to Connor, watching her. They continued to work on their relationship, but the distance between them seemed to grow, instead of disappear.

"They're coming," the young waiter whispered to us as stepped out of sight. I took a deep breath, eager to see Jules' face when she saw Connor. This was her dream proposal. Family and friends gathered to witness and celebrate the moment. It was both public and intimate, and utterly perfect for Jules.

Jake walked up with Jules on his arm, stealing my breath as I saw him in his tuxedo. He'd been the one to pick up Jules, having her believe they were attending a fancy police fundraiser I couldn't attend.

Her eyes found Connor immediately, and Jake let her go as she walked toward him, having eyes only for one another. He came around to me, sliding his arm around my waist as I leaned against him.

Connor took Jules' hands as he bent down on one knee.

"Jules, you are the woman I wish to spend my life with. You're the moon that reflects my light even when its dark. You are strong, beautiful, loving. Every day I have with you is a blessing, one I thank God for every moment I breathe. Life may not always be easy, but there is no one I would rather spend it with than you. Will you do me the honor of becoming my wife?"

Love shone on his face as he stared at her, and she smiled, radiant in his love.

"Yes, Connor. I would love to be your wife."

He took the ring from the box, sliding it on her finger. We clapped, sniffles all around as she kissed him. The music changed, and I laughed. Trust Connor to take me literally.

They swayed together, and I twisted around, wrapping my arms around Jake's neck.

"You are my sunshine?" he asked, one eyebrow raised quizzically.

"Jules told me once that Connor was the sun to her moon. I might have told him that."

"So, he decided their engagement song should be, 'You are my Sunshine'?"

"Apparently."

"Huh, guess it works."

"It's a good song."

We swayed to the music, the stars twinkling above as other couples joined us.

"I love you. I don't know if I can ever say those words enough."

"You can try." I smiled at him, my fingers tangling in the hair at his collar. "I'll never grow tired of hearing them."

"Whatever the future holds, we'll face it together. I promise."

I tucked my head into his shoulder, grateful I'd survived. A smile curled on my lips as I remembered the sight of our son. I glanced around at the people gathered together and knew this was the beginning, and the man holding me was my future.

Would you like to see another *Hidden* novel? More Jake and Addie, Connor and Jules, Carly and Danny, and Wade? Let me know on Facebook or my website, https://kristincoley.com/! I love hearing from my readers and would love to know what you think about another *Hidden* novel. I'm kind of curious myself to know if Carly winds up with Danny and what exactly is up with Wade?

Sign up for my newsletter to keep up with the latest giveaways, new releases and opportunities for advanced reader copies.

~Other books by Kristin Coley~
The Anderson Brothers Series:
Finding Ford
Chasing Colt
Loving Livie

The Hidden Series:
Hidden Truths
Hidden Lies

The Trinity Trilogy:
Unbound
Found
Unite – Tentative February 2017

Printed in Great Britain
by Amazon